St... **happin**... **I've done** ... ... **a man I can** ... **duty?'**

'You don't hate me, Stella. ... lie. And it wouldn't be like that, ...
'You told me once your dream was to be a human rights lawyer, to effect widesprea... change. Becoming my Queen would allow you to do that. You would be altering the course of history. Bringing happiness to a people who have suffered enough. Can you really tell me that's not worth it?'

Her lips pursed. 'Pulling out your trump card, Kostas? Now I *know* you're desperate.'

'We both know that isn't my trump card. We've proved we could be very good together. *More* than good.'

MARRYING HER ROYAL ENEMY

BY
JENNIFER HAYWARD

First Published in Great Britain 2016
By Mills & Boon, an imprint of HarperCollins*Publishers*
1 London Bridge Street, London, SE1 9GF

© 2016 Jennifer Hayward

ISBN: 978-0-263-91637-9

Jennifer Hayward has been a fan of romance since filching her sister's novels to escape her teenage angst. Her career in journalism and PR, including years of working alongside powerful, charismatic CEOs and travelling the world, has provided perfect fodder for the fast-paced, sexy stories she likes to write, always with a touch of humour. A native of Canada's East Coast, Jennifer lives in Toronto with her Viking husband and young Viking-in-training.

Visit the Author Profile page at millsandboon.co.uk for more titles.

A special thanks to Captain Steve Krotow, USN (ret.),
for his insight into naval aviation.
You were so helpful and fascinating!
Now I really want to land on a carrier someday.

And to my brother Andrew
for being the most awesome brainstorm partner.

CHAPTER ONE

So this was what freedom tasted like.

Princess Styliani Constantinides, or Stella, as she had been known since birth, lifted an exotic rum-based cocktail to her lips and took a sip, the contrasting bitter and sweet flavors of the spirits lingering on her tongue before blazing a fiery path down to her stomach, where they imbued an intense feeling of well-being.

The perfect combination for this particular moment as she sat in her friend Jessie's tiny, local bar on the west coast of Barbados, halfway around the world from her home in Akathinia, contemplating her future.

Sweet, given the burnout she'd been suffering from after the hundred-plus public appearances she'd done last year, in addition to her work chairing the boards of two international youth agencies. *Bitter* because her brother Nik had accused her of running away from the issue at hand.

As if it had been just yesterday she'd ditched her Swiss finishing school to spend a month in Paris when she'd thought the stifling formality of her studies might suck the very life out of her. As if every sacrifice she'd made since then had meant nothing...

"How's that?"

The testosterone-laden, dreadlocked bartender rested

his forearms on the gray-veined marble bar and cocked a thick, dark brow at her.

"On the nose." The smile she gave him was the first real one she'd managed in months. He offered a thumbs-up in return, then moved on to serve another customer.

Relaxing back in her stool, she cradled the tulip-shaped glass in her hands and studied the fiery jewel tones of the cocktail glowing in the fairy lights of the beachside bar. She deigned to disagree with her brother, the king. She was not, in fact, running, so much as drawing a line in the sand. She may have given up her childhood dream for her country and sacrificed the freedom that was like oxygen to her, but her brother's latest request was over the line. Untenable. Out of the question.

She wouldn't do it.

Her breath left her in a long, cathartic exhale. Pulling in another lungful of the salty ocean air, she felt her limbs loosen, the band of tension encircling her skull ease, the tightness in her chest unwind. The release of pressure unshackled something inside of her that had been knotted and twisted for weeks.

When was the last time she'd felt she could breathe? As if the forces conspiring to turn her life upside down were not in control, but *she* was. As if the insanity that had driven her to this Caribbean paradise had simply been a vexing nightmare that an airplane ticket purchased under an assumed name and a lifetime of skill in eluding her bodyguards could fix.

A smile curved her lips. It had been a compelling game. Almost as fun as the ones she and Nik had used to play on the palace staff. Convincing Darius, her ex–special ops bodyguard, to let her leave the palace alone and dropping an arch hint she was headed for a secret tryst, when, in fact, a man was the last thing she wanted in her life, had summoned a blush to the hardened serviceman's cheeks and an agreement to "overlook" her departure from the palace. Boarding a commercial flight in a Harvard T-shirt and sunglasses and making the getaway from the pink-sanded Mediterranean island paradise she called home had been even easier.

The only rain on her very slick parade had been the text from Nik. She'd sent him one to say she was fine, that she needed time to think. His blunt, admonishing reply had made her turn off her phone.

Her brother could, of course, find her if he wanted to. But she knew he wouldn't. Once her twin royal rebel, Nik knew the price it had cost her to clip her wings. He himself had made the ultimate sacrifice in taking their brother Athamos's place as king, giving up the life he'd loved in New York when Athamos had been killed in a tragic car accident that had rocked Akathinia. He would allow her this time to find her head, *herself. If* she even knew who she was anymore.

"Need a menu?" The bartender waved one at her.

"Please." There were no paparazzi lying in wait to chase her from the bar, no Darius watching her with eagle-eyed precision from ten feet away, nor did anyone have a clue who she was in jeans, a T-shirt and sunglasses. Since Jessie wouldn't be free until the dinner rush was over, she might as well eat and enjoy the superb sunset from one of the patio tables.

"I hear the calamari is spectacular."

The low, textured voice came from her right, delivered by the male who slid onto the stool beside her. She froze, breath jamming in her throat. The hairs on the back of her neck rose to attention, a sense of unreality washing over her. *It couldn't be.* Except that voice carrying a Carnelian accent, infused with a Western inflection, that richly flavored, deeply masculine tone, could belong to only one man.

Noooo. Every muscle in her body tensed in rejection, her heart shutting down in coordination with her breathing as the earthy, sensual scent of him slammed into her senses. Her toes curled in her shoes, ordering—*begging*—her to run. But she had never been, nor would she ever be, a coward, so she looked up at the king of Carnelia instead.

Tall and muscular, he dwarfed the stool he sat on, as if he went on forever, the sheer brawn of him riveting; *intimidating.* But what was perhaps more hazardous to a woman's health was how all that sheer masculine power was cloaked with a civilized veneer that had always set him apart from his savage of a father. That had once made her believe he was different.

Kostas Laskos lifted a hand to capture the bartender's attention, an unnecessary action when everyone in the bar was staring at him. The women because his hawkish, striking face, set off by his short-cropped black hair, was just that arresting. The men because anyone that dangerous was to be inspected and sized up immediately.

"The oldest Mount Gay you have," the king requested.

Diavole. Her stomach retracted in a visceral reaction only this man had ever been able to elicit. Stunning, as he had been the last time she'd seen him, in ceremonial uniform at the Independence Day ball in Akathinia, tonight in jeans and a shirt rolled up at the elbows, he was compelling in a way the sunset staining the sky outside was—an utterly unavoidable, spectacularly beautiful product of nature.

His long, powerful fingers claimed her attention as he lowered them to his side. He had lethal hands—ones that could snap a man's neck as easily as they had crushed her eighteen-year-old heart. Hands that purportedly seduced so skillfully that women lined up for him to do it, but she wouldn't know because he had saved his cruelest rejection for her.

Her teeth sank into her lower lip, the effects of him reverberating through her. He had kissed her with that beautiful, sensual mouth of his, the only soft part of Kostas that existed, to comfort her after her dreams had come crashing down around her. He had stripped her of her innocent defenses, shown her what true fire could look like, then walked away, making a mockery of her teenage idolization.

She *hated* him.

He was watching her, analyzing her every reaction to him in that deadly way of his. She forced herself to speak past the blood pounding in her ears. "Shouldn't you be home ruling over that band of ruffians you inherited, or did your jet run out of fuel?"

A corner of his mouth lifted. "You know why I'm here."

She set down her glass with a jerky movement, liquid sloshing precariously close to the sides. "Well, you can refuel and be on your way. I gave Nik my answer. I wouldn't marry you if you came with a dowry of a hundred billion euros."

"I think you have that the wrong way around."

"I think I don't. I'm the prize in this scenario, am I not? Or you wouldn't have flown halfway around the world to harass me."

"I wouldn't have had to if you'd given me the time I'd requested."

"I refused what was on offer."

His whiskey-soaked gaze glittered. "How can you

know what you don't want when you don't even know what's on offer?"

She pressed her fingers against her mouth. "Let's see... *Hmm.* A barbarian for a husband, living in the enemy's lair, a union with a man who didn't even have the guts to try to stop his father when he tried to take Akathinia? No, *thank* you."

His jaw tightened. "Watch yourself, Stella. You don't have all the facts."

"It's a year and a half too late. I no longer care." She pushed away from the bar and slid off the stool. "Go home, Kostas."

"Sit down." The words left his mouth with the fine edge of a scythe. "Do me the courtesy of hearing me out. The time for tantrums is long past."

Customers turned to stare. Jessie, who was seating a table, looked over, eyes widening as she took in the man beside her. Stella waved her off and sat down because she didn't want to cause a scene and blow her cover. *Not* because of the inherent command in the king's voice.

Kostas pinned his gaze on her. "Have dinner with me. Listen to what I have to say. I promise if you do, I will leave and accept whatever decision you make."

Accept whatever decision she made? Had he always been this arrogant? How could she once have thought herself so blindingly in love with him she'd willingly made a complete fool of herself over him?

Heat smoked through her, singeing her skin. *"Kala,"* she drawled in her most agreeable voice. "You're right. This conversation is long overdue. Why don't you order us a good bottle of Bordeaux, find a table, and we'll discuss it over dinner like two civilized adults?"

She slid off the stool and sashayed toward the washrooms.

* * *

Kostas knew the moment Stella turned on her heel that she wasn't coming back. He knew *her*. Had known her since childhood, when the royal families of Akathinia and Carnelia had crossed paths at official celebrations, at the dozens of royal occasions that marked the season in the Mediterranean. His family had had a measure of respectability then, as his father's tendency toward a dictatorial rule had been less pronounced.

He had watched Stella grow from an undeniably attractive teenager into a spirited, often recalcitrant young woman who spent so much of her time flaunting the rules he wasn't sure she could see past her insurgency. Except of late. The past few years had seen the Akathinian princess turn herself into a respected global philanthropist, her rebellious edge muted if not entirely eliminated.

And for that, he was glad. It was her will he had always respected, found himself irresistibly drawn to. Her strength of character. It was a quality he required in a wife, a woman who could accomplish extraordinary things with him—change the very fabric of a nation that had suffered greatly. Few would have the courage to take on the challenge he was about to offer her. Stella had been born with it.

He caught the proprietor's attention, secured a private table outside on the edge of the patio, then returned inside to lean against the wall opposite the washrooms, arms crossed over his chest. When Stella emerged and headed directly for the exit, he cleared his throat.

"I thought you might need help finding the table," he offered in as benign a tone as she had drawn him in with. "Château Margaux okay?"

Her eyes widened, then narrowed, a series of emotions flashing across her arresting face as she formulated an alternate game plan. "Lovely," she announced, swishing past him into the restaurant.

He followed, a surge of amusement filling him as he contemplated her better-than-average backside, set off to perfection in formfitting blue jeans. He couldn't remember the last time he'd felt alive, awake to the zest of a life he'd lost his taste for. It figured Stella would be the one to snap him out of it.

Guiding her to the table on the patio with his fingertips at her elbow, he held her chair out for her. She sat down, allowing him to push in the chair. He deliberately let his fingers brush her shoulders as he lifted his hands away, eliciting a visible flinch from the princess. *A test.* He recorded it with satisfaction. She wished it to be hate, but he knew it was anything but.

He fixed his attention on the woman sitting across from him while he waited for their server to uncork the impressive bottle of Bordeaux. Devoid of makeup, with her hair pulled back into a tight ponytail, the bold, strong lines of her face were a challenge in themselves. Not classically beautiful, but unforgettable when paired with her ice-blue eyes and blond hair.

Where every other woman had eventually faded to a blurry replication of the last, Stella had remained unique. The one he couldn't group with all the rest. The one his twenty-three-year-old self had somehow resisted with an impressive display of self-control. *Just.*

The waiter left the wine to breathe. Kostas laced his fingers together on the table and addressed the land mine that lay between them. "I'm sorry about Athamos. I know how much you loved him. I understand the grief you and your family must be going through."

"Do you?" She lifted her chin, fixing those spectacular blue eyes on him. "I don't think you could possibly

understand the grief we feel because you are alive, Kostas, and Athamos is dead."

He drew in a breath at the direct hit. He had expected it. Deserved it. Had spent every waking moment since the night Athamos had died wishing he could turn back time. Wishing he could bring Stella's brother, the former crown prince of Akathinia, back to his family. But he couldn't. The events of that night would always be a waking nightmare for him. A reminder of his flaws. All he could do was forgive himself for his mistakes and attempt to move on before he destroyed himself, too. With a country resting its hopes on him, that wasn't an option.

He held her cold, bitter gaze. "He was a friend as much as a rival, you know that. Our relationship was complex. I need to take responsibility for what happened that night, but both Athamos and I agreed to that race. We both made bad decisions."

Fire disintegrated the ice in her eyes. "Yes, but *you* were the ringleader. I've heard the stories about you two in flight school—they're legendary. You egged him on until neither of you could see straight past your obsession to win. But you weren't collecting points to be top dog that night, you were gambling with your lives. How can I forgive you for that knowing Athamos was following in your trail? In your suicidal *jet wash*?"

"Because you need to," he growled. "Because bitterness won't solve anything. I can't bring him back, Stella. I would if I could. You need to forgive me so we can move on."

"It's too late for forgiveness."

He closed his hand over hers on the table. She yanked it away, glaring at him.

"What was so important you couldn't have come to us and explained what happened? What was so *impera-*

tive you needed to walk away without putting us out of our misery?"

"I should have." He closed his eyes, searching for the right words. "What happened that night rocked me...shattered me. I needed time to process what had happened. To pick up the pieces..."

"And that was more important than the precious peace and democracy you preach?" She fired the words at him, her hand slicing through the air. "While you were *finding* yourself, we were living in fear, *terrified* your father would annex Akathinia back into the Catharian Islands. How could you *not* have intervened?"

His fingers curled around the edge of the table. "My father was the king. Short of overthrowing him, spearheading a mutiny against my own flesh and blood, the only thing I could do was try to reason with him. It wasn't working near the end. He was losing his mental faculties, suffering from dementia. I had to bide my time until I took control."

"So you put yourself into a self-imposed exile?"

"I went to Tibet."

"Tibet?" Her eyes widened. "You went to live with the monks?"

"Something like that."

She stared at him as if searching for some sign he was joking. When he said nothing, she sat back in her chair, eyes bleak. "Did your *sojourn* afford you the forgiveness you craved? The absolution? Or perhaps it was *peace* you were looking for. Lord knows we've all been searching for that. We didn't even have a body to bury."

He brought his back teeth together. *"Enough,* Stella."

"Or *what*?" She tossed her hair over her shoulder. "I am not your *subject,* Kostas. You can't fly in here, interrupt the first vacation I've had in years and order me around like your dictator of a father loved to do. You're the one walking on very thin ground right about now."

He was. He knew it. "Tell me how I can make this right," he growled. "You know we need to."

The waiter arrived to pour their wine. Dispensing the dark red Bordeaux into their glasses, he took one look at their faces and melted away. Stella took a sip, then cradled the glass between her palms, eyes on his. "What happened that night? Why did you race?"

His heart began a slow thud in his chest. Every detail, every minute fragment of that night was imprinted on his brain. He had promised himself he wasn't ever going there again, and yet if he didn't, Stella would walk out on him, he knew that with certainty.

"Athamos and I met a Carnelian woman named Cassandra Liatos. We both had feelings for her. She was torn, liked us both. We decided to settle it with a car race through the mountains—the winner got the girl."

Her jaw dropped. "You had a *pink-slip race*, except the prize was a woman?"

His mouth flattened. "I'm not sure that's a fair comparison. One of us had to back off. Cassandra couldn't make the call, so we did."

"So she was merely a pawn in the game between two future kings?" A dazed look settled over her face. She rubbed her fingertips against her temples and shook her head. "That wasn't my brother. He didn't treat women as objects. What was *wrong* with him?"

His gaze fell away from hers. "It was not a rational night."

"No, it was a deadly one." The rasp in her voice brought his eyes back up to hers. "Where is Cassandra now? Were you with her after Athamos died?"

"No. It was…impossible to move on from there."

Stella looked out at the sunset darkening the horizon to a deep burnt orange. The convulsing of her throat, the slow deliberate breaths she took, told him how hard she was fighting for control. When she eventually returned her gaze to his, she was all hard-as-ice composed.

"Are you *done*? Have you said all you need to say? Because if you think I'm going to marry you after hearing that, Kostas—sign on to be another one of your pawns— you are out of your mind."

He leaned forward, resting his forearms on the table. "It was a *mistake*. I made a mistake, one I will pay for the rest of my life. What I am proposing between us is a partnership, not a chance for me to lord it over you. An opportunity to restore peace and democracy in the Ionian Sea. To heal the wounds we have all suffered."

Her mouth curled. "So I should *save* you after everything you've done? Allow myself to be used as a symbol you can flaunt to the world in some PR exercise you are undertaking to restore Carnelia's credibility?"

The animosity emanating from her shocked him. "When did you become so cynical? So unforgiving? Where is the woman who would have done anything to fight for a better world?"

"I *am* fighting for a better world. Every day I do that with my work. It's *you* who seems to have lost your compass. *You* are not the man I once knew. That man would have stayed and fought your father tooth and nail. *He* would not have jumped ship."

"You're right," he said harshly, bitter regret staining his heart. "I'm not the man I was. I am a realist, not an idealist. It's the only thing that's going to save my country from the mess it's in."

She regarded him over the rim of her glass. "And how do you intend to do that? Save Carnelia?"

"My father has driven the approval ratings for the monarchy to historic lows. I plan to hold elections to turn Carnelia into a constitutional monarchy in the fall, which will include a confirmation by the people they wish the monarchy to stay in place. There is a very real possibility, however, before I can do that, the military junta who backed my father will seize control. You marrying me, joining Akathinia and Carnelia together in a symbolic alliance, would be a powerful demonstration of the future I can give to my people if they afford me the opportunity. A vision of peace and freedom."

An air of incredulity surrounded her. "You're asking me to marry you, to walk into the enemy's lair, where a powerful military faction might take control at any moment, and transform a country, a government, with you?"

"Yes. You have the courage, the strength and the compassion to help me take Carnelia forward into the future it deserves."

Her eyes flashed. "And what about me? Am I supposed to lay my happiness down on the altar as I've done everything else? Marry a man I can't stand for the sake of duty?"

He shook his head. "You don't hate me, Stella. You know that's a lie. And it wouldn't be like that. You told me once your dream was to become a human rights lawyer, to effect widespread change. Becoming my queen would allow you to do that. You would be altering the course of history, bringing happiness to a people who have suffered enough. Can you really tell me that's not worth it?"

Her lips pursed. "Pulling out your trump card, Kostas? Now I know you're desperate."

"We both know that isn't my trump card. We've proved we could be very good together. *More* than good."

A deep red flush stained her chest, rising up to claim

her cheeks. "That was ten years ago and it was just a kiss."

"One *hell* of a kiss. Enough you jumped into my bed in flimsy lingerie and waited for me until one o'clock in the morning, while the entire party thought you were ill."

A choked sound left her throat. "You are such a gentleman for bringing that up."

"No," he countered softly, "I was that when I tossed you out. You were Athamos's little sister, Stella. *Eighteen.* I was the son of the dictator. Kissing you was the height of stupidity when I knew the pedestal you put me on. I tried to end it there, but you wouldn't take no for an answer. Sometimes cruelty is kindness in its most rudimentary form."

Her sapphire eyes blazed a brilliant blue beam at him. "You should have spared me the pity kiss, then."

"It was far more complicated than that between us and you know it." She had been wrecked by her parents' refusal to allow her to accept the Harvard Law School admission she'd been granted, where Nik had studied. Devastated, as her dream had evaporated. *He* had not been prepared for the chemistry that had exploded between them.

"Would you have preferred I'd taken you?" He held her stormy gaze. "Walked away with a precious piece of you and broken your heart?"

"No," she huffed, fingernails digging into the armrests of her chair. "You did me a favor. And now that we've confirmed you're a heartless piece of work I'd never consider marrying, I think we've said all there is to say."

He studied the emotion cascading through her beautiful eyes, regret sinking through him. He had hurt her. Perhaps more than he'd thought.

She stood up in a whirlwind of motion, snatching up

her purse, pushing back her chair, as if a hurricane was sweeping down the Atlantic headed straight for them.

"Breaking our deal?" he drawled.

"The deal was to hear you out. Suddenly, I find myself without an appetite."

He stood, then reached into his pocket, pulled out his wallet and extracted a card from the marina where he was staying. She flinched as he tucked it into the front pocket of her jeans. "Don't make this decision because you hate me, Stella. Make it for what you believe in. Make it for Akathinia. If the military isn't handcuffed, they will seek to finish the job they started when they took that Akathinian ship last year. Lives will be lost."

Her chin dropped, her lithe body tense, caught in the middle of a storm. "I know you," he murmured. "You'll do the right thing."

"No, you don't." She shook her head slowly, a wealth of emotion throbbing in those blue eyes. "You don't know anything about me."

CHAPTER TWO

KOSTAS COULDN'T KNOW her because she clearly didn't know herself at this moment in time. The fact that she was even *entertaining* his proposition was ludicrous.

Stella paced the terrace of Jessie's oceanfront villa, smoke coming out of her ears. How *dare* he come here? How *dare* he throw that guilt trip at her? She had come to Barbados to get her head together, to figure out what she wanted to be. Instead, he had dumped the weight of two countries on her shoulders; issued that parting salvo that had her head spinning…

If the military isn't handcuffed, they will seek to finish the job they started when they took that Akathinian ship last year.

Her stomach plummeted, icy tendrils of fear clutching her insides. Five crew members had died when a renegade Carnelian commander had taken an Akathinian ship during routine military exercises in the waters between Akathinia and Carnelia last year. If Kostas lost control of Carnelia and the military seized power, Akathinia was in danger.

But to marry him to protect her country? Commit herself to a union of duty, something she'd vowed never to do?

She halted her incessant pacing. Leaned her forearms

on the railing of the terrace and looked out at the dark mass of the sea, a painful knot forming in the pit of her stomach. At least she knew the truth about Athamos now. It didn't explain why Cassandra Liatos had been so special that he'd engaged in a death race with Kostas over her—why he'd been so foolish as to throw his life away over someone who didn't know her own mind.

Unless he'd loved her...

Frustration curled her fingers tight. *Had he?* Was that the answer to the mystery that plagued her? She wanted to pound her fists against the big barrel of her brother's chest and demand an answer, but Athamos wasn't here. Wouldn't ever be here again.

Bitter regret swept through her, hot tears burning her eyes, threatening to spill over into the sorrow she'd refused to allow herself to feel lest it disintegrate what was left of her. Somehow she had to let him go. She just didn't know how.

She was pacing the deck again when Jessie came home, high heels clicking on the wood, a bottle of wine and two glasses in her hands.

"What is *Kostas* doing here? He nearly blew your cover. I had to convince a regular you were a friend from church."

She could use a little higher guidance right about now. "He wants me to marry him."

Jessie's eyes bulged out of her head. *"Marry him?"*

"Open the wine."

Her friend uncorked the bottle, poured two glasses and handed her one.

She took a sip. Rested her glass on the railing. "It would be a political match."

"Why?"

"I am the symbolic key to peace and democracy in the

Ionian Sea. A way for Akathinia and Carnelia to heal. A vision of the way forward."

"Are you expected to walk on water, too?"

A smile curved her lips. "It would be a powerful statement if Kostas and I were to marry."

Jessie fixed her with an incredulous look. "You can't commit yourself to a marriage of duty. Look what it did to your mother. It almost destroyed her."

All of them. Her parents' marriage may have been a political union, but her mother had loved her father. Unfortunately, her father had not been capable of loving anyone, not his wife nor his children. The king's chronic affairs had created a firestorm in the press and destroyed her family in the process.

"Kostas worries about the military junta that backed his father. He plans to hold elections to create a constitutional monarchy in the fall, but he's afraid the military will seize control before then if he doesn't send a powerful message of change."

"And you being the poster child of global democracy will give him that."

"Yes."

Jessie eyed her. "You aren't actually considering this?"

Silence.

Jessie took a sip of her wine. Leaned back against the railing as she contemplated her. "Can we talk about the elephant in the room? You were in love with him, Stella. Mad about him. If this isn't you repeating history, I don't know what is."

"It was a childish crush. It meant nothing."

Jessie's mouth twisted. "You two spent an entire summer with eyes only for each other. It was predestined between you two… Then you finally act on it and he slams the door in your face."

She shook her head. "It was never going to happen. It was too complicated."

"Does that discount you measuring every other man by him? This is *me*, hon. I knew you back then. I know you now. You looked shell-shocked when he walked into that bar. You still do."

"I can control it."

"Can you? You once thought the sun rose and set over him. He was the newest superhero to join the party, sent to rescue all of us from the bad guys."

What an apt description of her teenage infatuation with Kostas... Of the heroic status she'd afforded him for his determination to bring a better democratic way to his people. Her belief he was the only one who could recognize the bitter, alienating loneliness that had consumed her, because, she'd been sure, he'd carried it with him, too.

But that had simply been a manifestation of her youthful infatuation, she conceded, her chest searing. Her desperate need to be understood, *loved*, rather than seeing the real flesh-and-blood man he had been.

"I know his flaws now," she said, lifting her gaze to Jessie's. "His major fault lines..." She no longer harbored the airbrushed image of him that had once steered her so wrong.

"The thing is," she mused, her subconscious ramblings bubbling over into conscious thought, "I haven't been happy in a long time, Jess. I've been restless, caged in a box I can't seem to get out of. Everything about my life is charmed, *perfect*, and yet I'm miserable."

Jessie gave her a rueful look. "I was working my way around to that. But why? You do amazing work. *Meaningful* work. Doesn't it give you satisfaction?"

"Yes, but it's not truly mine. Other than my support for

the disarmament issue, it's the sanitized, gilded, photo-op version of philanthropy the palace directs." She shook her head. "You know I've always felt I have a higher calling. The ability to effect widespread change because of who I am, the power I have. And yet every time I've tried to spread my wings, I've been reined in. Athamos and Nik have taken precedence. *I* was the one left to toe the line."

Jessie was silent. "I hear what you're saying," she said finally. "But this is *big*, Stella. Irreversible. If you marry him, you're going to be queen. You will be taking on a nation. You're going to be walking into a very delicate situation with no real control."

But weren't those the kind of challenges that made her feel alive, despite the inherent risk involved? Wasn't this what she'd been craving all her life, a chance to make her mark?

She and Jessie talked late into the night. When her friend finally pleaded exhaustion and drifted off to bed, Stella stayed on the terrace, tucked in a chair, the fat half crescent of a moon, tossed in a sea of stars, her silent companion.

She didn't question her ability to do what Kostas was asking of her. She'd walked through war zones to promote peace in countries where young people were the innocent victims of conflict. She'd met and challenged tribal leaders to find a better way than destroying each other. What she was afraid of was *Kostas*. What he could do to her in a political marriage with her as his pawn.

Tonight had proved, a decade later, she was far from immune to him. In fact, it had illustrated the opposite; revealed the origins of her stunningly bad mistake with Aristos Nicolades last year.

She had worked her way through a series of men whom she'd discarded one after another without allowing any of them to get close. When that had proved unsatisfactory, she'd fixed her sights on Aristos to prove she could win a man every bit as unattainable as Kostas; as elusive and undeniably fascinating. She'd sought to exorcise the ghost of her most painful rejection, to prove she was *worth* more than that. Instead, Aristos had broken her heart and, worse, fallen head over heels in love with her sister and married her.

She wrapped her arms around her knees and hugged them to her chest, the pang that went through her only a faint echo of what it once had been, because she'd anesthetized it, marked it as mindless self-pity.

She was destined to be alone. Had accepted that love was unattainable to her. That she'd been too badly scarred too many times to view the concept as anything but a destructive force. Which would almost make the suggestion of a political match bearable. Practical. If it was with anyone but Kostas.

Tying her fate to a man who could destroy her, if the forces threatening to splinter Carnelia apart didn't do it first, seemed like another bad decision in a long list of many. *Unless* she neutralized his effect on her.

If she was to do this—marry Kostas—and survive, she would need to bury her feelings for him in a deep, untouchable place where he couldn't use them against her.

The question was…could she?

"The princess is here to see you, Your Highness."

Kostas looked up from the intelligence briefing he was reviewing, his heart climbing into his throat. It had been two days since he'd thrown all his cards at Stella, hoping she'd see the light. Two days with no response. Due to return to Carnelia tomorrow for a regional summit of leaders, he'd started to think his penchant for risk taking had been his downfall. That he had overrated his negotiating skills when it came to a princess who harbored a very personal anger toward him.

He betrayed not one ounce of the relief flooding through him as he nodded to his aide, Takis. "I'll go up."

Taking the steps to the upper deck of his old friend Panos Michelakos's yacht, anchored in Carlisle Bay while its owner took care of business in the West Indies, he found Stella standing at the railing of the impressive seventy-foot boat, looking out at the ocean.

She was silhouetted against the dying rays of the sun, her hair, the color of rich honey, hanging loose down her back. Her slim body was encased in a white skirt and caramel-colored tank top. She looked every inch the cool, sophisticated golden girl she was reputed to be, except he knew from experience Stella was anything but cold. She brought passion to everything she did.

He was fairly sure the image of her in bloodred lingerie, curled up in his bed at the Akathinian palace, would forever be imprinted on his brain. Stored there to torture him with the memory of the one woman he had never allowed himself to have; the one who had never left his head.

A slow curl of heat unraveled inside of him as the erotic image painted itself across his brain. It had been late, the early morning, when he'd climbed the stairs to his room after a palace party, head hazy from too many shots of *tsipouro*. He'd let himself into his suite unaware anyone else was there, stripped off his clothes, left them in a pile on the floor and collapsed onto the king-size bed.

It was only when his splayed arm had touched silky soft female skin that he'd become aware he wasn't alone. He'd thought maybe he had drunk too much and dreamed up the lingerie-covered Stella until she'd started talking, telling him he was the most exciting man she'd ever met, that their kiss earlier in the library had been incredible and she wanted him to be her first.

His twenty-three-year-old brain had nearly exploded. She was every red-blooded male's fantasy come true with her high, perfect breasts and mile-long legs. His body had definitely not been in tune with his head. She'd been too innocent, too pure, too full of her ambitions to change the world for a man caught in a struggle to define himself as different from his autocrat of a father to ever pursue. A man unsure he could ever live up to the lofty ideals she'd built around him.

Somewhere in his liquor-soaked brain, he'd summoned up the sanity to scoop her up, carry her to the door and deposit her on the other side, telling her to go kick sand in her own playground. He'd been sure someday the shattered look on her face would be worth it when she realized he'd spared her a broken heart. That women, for him, were fleeting pleasures meant to be enjoyed, then discarded in the must-win, must-conquer existence that had characterized his life.

But after that night, he sensed his callousness had dug far deeper than he'd believed in a tough, resilient Stella. That his need to underscore he was not the man for her, not the man for any woman in their right mind, had hurt her deeply.

She sensed his presence before he revealed himself. Turning, hands curling around the rail, a charge rocketed through her. Her soon-to-be fiancé was studying her with an intense curiosity in his hawk-like gaze that seemed to strip the layers from her skin, deconstructing every one of the protective barriers she'd come armed with.

Her chin dipped as he moved toward her. "Planning your next move, Kostas?"

"Admiring you. You still have the power to stop me in my tracks."

Her stomach folded in on itself, a renegade wave of heat spreading through her in places that needed to remain ice-cold. "No need for flattery," she said, injecting some of that much-needed, cool composure into her tone. "You know why I'm here."

"Honesty," he countered as he came to a halt in front of her, "is something you will always get from me, Stella. Whether you like what I have to say or not."

Another veiled reference to his humiliating rejection of her? A current of awareness zigzagged through her as she took him in. In a short-sleeved shirt and trousers today, the fading light of the sun illuminating the deep lines etching his eyes and mouth, there was a life experience imprinted on the hard contours of his face that lent him a somberness she didn't recall. A *knowledge*.

If those deeply embedded marks that had taken purchase on him made her wonder what the forces had been that had changed him so, had driven him to Tibet on a soul-searching expedition, she pushed that curiosity aside. She was here to negotiate her future.

"I'm good with honesty," she drawled, holding his dark gaze. "It's always been my forte. Along with sticking to my principles and reaping the messes I sow."

He ignored the gibe. "What changed your mind?"

"You were right. Notorious dissident that I am, I cannot turn my back on our two countries. Nor on my big dreams, because yes, I do still have them. But there are conditions attached to my becoming your queen."

He leaned against the rail and folded his arms over his chest. "Let's hear them."

"I will not be a figurehead...smothered by the patriarchal establishment. You will give me real power and status."

"Do you have any advance thoughts?"

"A seat on your executive council."

His gaze flickered. "That would be most...*unusual*."

"Say yes, Kostas, or this isn't happening."

He gave her a long look. "*Kala*. You can have a seat on the council. But I warn you it will not be an easy ride. Akathinia may be enlightened, but Carnelia is still stuck in the Dark Ages."

"I like a challenge. Clearly. Second, I will continue my work with the current organizations I support unless my schedule proves to be excessive."

"I have no problem with that. You do great work. What you *cannot* do is waltz around active war zones. It's too risky."

Heat lanced through her. "I do not *waltz*, Kostas. The photograph of me with those children raised millions of dollars toward the support of a regional disarmament treaty."

He tilted his head. "An unfortunate choice of words. But the fact remains, I need my queen alive."

Not because he cared, because she was of *value* to him.

"Third," she continued, "you will not take a mistress. Should you do so, I will have the power to divorce you immediately. It will not require a decree signed by government."

"I'm not your father, Stella. I have no intention of indulging in affairs. Why would I when I have a woman like you in my bed?"

Her gaze rested on his. "Speaking of which, this will be a political marriage. As such, I will not be under duress to sleep with you."

His gaze narrowed. "That might be a problem given the fact I need to produce an heir *quickly* in order to secure the Laskos line. Also, your fourth point seems to be in direct contradiction to your third. I can't have a mistress, but we aren't going to have sex?"

She waved a hand at him. "The heir—we can make that happen."

"How does that work?" He took a step closer, dwarfing her with his height and breadth. "We have *conjugal* visits? I seek you out when the *temperature* is right?"

She tilted her head back to look up at him, every cell in her body going on high alert at the proximity of such blatant masculinity. "Something like that."

A dark glitter filled his gaze. "Setting yourself up as a martyr, Stella? The sacrificial lamb sent to slaughter for the king's pleasure?"

Her chin lifted. "I would not be the first princess to sacrifice myself to the call of duty. History is littered with them. We are valued for our beauty and poise, our *compassion* and *empathy*, but in the end are viewed as nothing more than glorified broodmares."

He gave her a long look. "I am offering you far more than that. This would be a true partnership."

"Along with the heir you so *urgently* require."

He flicked a hand at her. "What happens when you are not acting as my *broodmare*? When I have normal male urges?"

Her cheeks flamed at the erotic image that spurred in her head. She *knew* what he looked like from that night she'd waited for him in his bed...knew how heart-stoppingly virile he was in every respect. It made the blood coursing through her veins fizzle with heat. Singe her skin.

Diavole, but this was not how this was supposed to

go. She lifted her chin higher, a belligerent expression on her face. "That's not for me to figure out, Kostas. That's *your* job."

"Is it?" His gaze touched her fiery cheeks. "I think when you let go of the past, when you finally forgive me, when you acknowledge how good we are together, we will be as potent a match in the bedroom as we will be ruling my country."

"No," she said, even as a pulse of electricity ran between them, magnifying the sizzle in her blood. "That isn't going to happen. Women are objects to you. I am a means to an end. I would be stupid to forget that and cede power to you."

"You will be my *wife*, the woman by my side, not an object." His dark lashes arced over his cheeks. "And who said you would be ceding power? Just because I walked away from you that night didn't mean I didn't want you, Stella. That I haven't replayed that scenario in my head with a far different outcome. You would have equally as much power over me if we went to bed together, maybe more."

Her stomach muscles coiled. It was a seductive, beguiling thought to imagine he might want her. That her desire for him hadn't been as one-sided as she'd imagined it to be. That by exploring that revelation, she might wipe away the rejection that stung even now in a place that had never healed. But her head, the part of her she was operating with now, realized his tactics for what they were. *Negotiation. Manipulation.*

She lifted her chin. "It will be an act, conceiving your heir. Nothing more. I've lost my taste for megalomaniacs housed in beautiful packages."

"Megalomaniacs?"

"Yes—*you*."

He studied her for a moment. "Are you including Aristos Nicolades in this esteemed group?"

She lifted a brow. "Following my love life, Kostas? Aristos was simply the last kick at the can." Her voice took on a nonchalance that hid the steel underpinning her insides. "I've decided to make myself as impenetrable as you when it comes to relationships, as *unaffected*, because I've found, in the end, it's just not worth it."

He frowned. "That's not you, Stella. You live by your passion."

"Not anymore I don't. You should be happy about my new outlook, by the way. It's the only reason I'm marrying you."

"That and your desire to do the immense amount of good I know you will."

"Don't patronize." She took a step back because oxygen was necessary for breathing and she couldn't do that near him. "I'm already on board if you agree to the conditions I've laid out."

He nodded. "Agreed. Shall we go over next steps, then?"

Her head spun. *This was actually happening.* "Go ahead."

"I fly back to Carnelia tomorrow for a summit of regional leaders. It would be ideal if you accompanied me so we can make the engagement announcement and begin preparations for the wedding."

Tomorrow? She had been craving this time to herself so badly.

He read her dismay. "General Houlis, the chief architect behind the military junta, has put his campaign into motion, marshaling strength behind the scenes. His support is by no means solid—he still has a long way to go. We need to neutralize him while we can."

"I'm assuming the coming elections will be a major weapon at your disposal?"

"Yes. I will announce them at the summit this week. There will be a large media contingent in attendance. Nik will also be there. We will provide a united front."

"And our engagement? Do we announce that before or after?"

"I will double-check with the palace PR team, but I was thinking this coming Friday. Start the week with a bang at the conference, end the week with an equally strong commitment toward the future."

"And the wedding? When would that happen?"

"Within two months. Six weeks, I'm thinking. Those who can make it, make it."

"Six weeks?"

"The events team will make it happen. You just need to show up."

Like her role in all of this. A chess piece to be moved around at will.

His expression turned conciliatory. "I know it's traditional for the engagement party to happen in Akathinia, but in this instance, I think it needs to be in Carnelia with all the key figures in attendance.

Her mother was going to have a fit. A deviant streak reveled in the thought. She enjoyed every opportunity she had to push her aloof mother out of her comfort zone. A latent lashing out against her childhood perhaps, at the attention she'd never received.

"That's fine." She watched her dream sabbatical fly out the metaphorical window. She could hardly relax on a beach now knowing what was ahead of her.

"Good." He reached into his pocket and pulled out a ring. Caught off guard, she was blinded by its brilliance. A square-cut diamond set in an exquisite platinum filigree, it dazzled in the sunlight. Upon closer inspection, she saw it had the Carnelian coat of arms interwoven on both sides.

"You were that sure of me?"

"Hopeful. This was my mother's ring. One of the few remaining mementos I have of her."

Her chest tightened, a sandpapery feeling invading her throat. "She died when you were very young, I remember."

"When I was four. I have no real memories of her."

She studied his impassive expression. What must it have been like to grow up without any warmth in his life? With only his universally despised tyrant of a father to guide him? Had he had someone else to confide in, to love him—a grandmother, a godmother? She couldn't remember him talking of one. Or had he always been alone?

Athamos had once remarked Kostas was the only man he knew who could look alone in the middle of a crowd. It was something she'd never forgotten. How could she?

"Your hand," Kostas prompted, pulling her back into the moment.

She held her hand out, her fingers trembling ever so slightly. He slid the ring on, his big hand engulfing hers. The enormity of what she was about to do lodged in her throat as she stared at the stone blazing on her finger. It was a ring that not only symbolized the commitment she was making to Kostas, but also the weight of a nation that now lay squarely on her shoulders.

Kostas held her gaze in his dark, unfathomable one. "*Efharisto*, Stella. *Thank you.* I promise you won't regret this. We will make a powerful team. We will give Carnelians the future they deserve."

His energy pulsed through her. Sank into the very heart of her. Her future was now inexorably intertwined with a man she had vowed to hate, a man for whom she now realized her feelings were far more complex than she'd ever anticipated. But there was no looking back now. It was done.

CHAPTER THREE

THE DAYS FOLLOWING Stella's return to Akathinia passed in a blur, likely a good thing given the magnitude of what she'd committed herself to. She knew her decision to marry Kostas had been the right one, knew this was the challenge she had been looking for. It was the *noise* that was getting to her.

Everyone seemed to have an opinion on her upcoming nuptials to the king of Carnelia, from her hairdresser, who pronounced him "a real man among the current flock of pseudo-men," to her sister, Aleksandra, who agreed with her hairdresser, referring to Kostas as "one sexy hunk of a man," to the celebrity press, who'd dubbed their pairing "the most exciting thing to happen to royalty in decades. Camelot has come to Carnelia."

The traditional media, on the other hand, Kostas's harshest critics, were taking a wait-and-see approach. Not all of them were convinced King Idas's son, the thirty-two-year-old Oxford-educated proponent of democracy, could turn his legacy around. Rumblings of military discontent were rippling across the country, approval ratings for the monarchy were down and all bets were off as to whether Kostas could win the hearts and minds of Carnelians.

But there was also hope. The Carnelian people seemed

guardedly optimistic, as spontaneous parties broke out in the streets as the first elections in the country's history were announced for the fall. Those celebrations continued with the news of the king's forthcoming match to the elder princess of Akathinia. For the great majority, she appeared the bright, promising light Kostas had painted, but for others she was an unknown quantity in a culture historically closed to outsiders. *Not* a Carnelian.

That would have to be overcome, she thought grimly as she flew to London for an official appearance the week before her engagement party. The future of a country, the self-determination of its people, depended on it, though they were so wounded at the moment, they weren't sure what they wanted.

The oppressive media coverage dogged her as she attended a charity luncheon in support of one of the major hospital's cancer units. What started out as a peaceful affair was hijacked by the news of her upcoming nuptials. Irritation chasing a beat up her spine, she apologized to her hostess. It was only a taste of the wedding madness, she knew, and it left her in an exceedingly cranky mood as she returned to Akathinia for a dress fitting with her sister-in-law, Sofía, and sister, Alex. A designer who was making her name on the world stage, Sofía was creating both her engagement party and wedding dresses.

"What do you think about this?" Sofía held up a sensational sapphire-hued backless satin gown in the bright light of her palace workshop at the front of the white Maltese stone Akathinian palace.

"Too obvious."

Sofía returned the dress to the rack and pulled out a white chiffon gown for her inspection.

"Too virginal."

Her sister-in-law flicked through the row of dresses and held up an elegant, midnight blue lace number.

She shook her head. "Just…not right."

Alex eyed her. "What are you, Goldilocks?"

At least there was a happy ending to that story. She ran a hand through her hair. "Sorry, I know I'm being a pain. It's been a bad week."

Sofía folded the dress over her arm. "You don't have to do this, you know. Nothing has been done that can't be undone."

Her sister-in-law should know. She'd been an ambitious, career-driven dress-shop owner in Manhattan before she'd fallen in love with Stella's brother, been swept up in romance and taken the unlikely path of becoming queen. But the road to happiness hadn't been an easy one for her and Nik.

"I'm doing the right thing." She said the words more vehemently than she felt them at the moment.

"For you or for your country?"

"For both."

Alex stayed quiet and she knew why. Her sister was blissfully happy with Aristos, who'd mellowed out from his jungle-cat personality to something approaching civility of late. Stella was happy for her, she really was, but it was like being slapped in the face with her own romantic futility every time she saw them together.

A knock on the door brought their heads up. Her brother strolled in, jacket over his arm, tie loose. He gave his wife a kiss, then glanced at the dress rack. "How's it going?"

Alex made a face. "How's it *not* going, you mean."

Nik took in Stella's dark look. "Can you give us a second?"

His wife and Alex left, clearly happy for a breather.

Her brother turned his ever-perceptive gaze on her. "Everything okay?"

"Never better."

"This was your decision, Stella."

"It's not that." She waved a hand at him. "I needed a challenge like this. I was dying inside going through the motions. It's this media circus that's getting to me. You'd think I'd solved world hunger instead of getting engaged."

"Think of it as good for Carnelia. People are excited."

"I know." She raked a hand through her hair. Strode to the window to look out at the glittering, sun-dappled Ionian Sea, across which her fiancé was attempting to manage the media firestorm he'd created. She wondered how he was doing. She'd talked to him on the phone a few times, but she'd mostly been working with Takis, his personal aide, on logistics, while Kostas attempted to hold a faltering country together.

"Kostas is a good man. Survivor's guilt is a hell of a thing to deal with. Give him some leeway."

She turned around. "You absolve him of any responsibility?"

"I have chosen to let go. You should, too."

She wasn't sure she was as enlightened as he was.

"I wanted to mention something else. Darius is going to accompany you to Carnelia. Permanently."

"I can't ask him to do that—he lives here."

"He wants to go. His loyalty to you has always been unquestionable."

She adored Darius. He'd kept her sane at times when it felt as if her life was just too *much*. "Does Kostas know about this?"

"He's in full agreement. I trust Kostas implicitly—he *will* take care of you. It's when he's not there I want an Akathinian, a known quantity, with you."

"Why? You think I'm in danger?"

"I think it's a smart precaution. You're walking into a very tricky political situation."

She didn't like how he hadn't answered the question. But then she'd known taking on this challenge was full of risk.

"Kala." Fine.

Nik's gaze softened. "I think you're very courageous to do this, Stella. I'm proud of you. Remember you are not alone. You are never alone. We're with you every step of the way."

Her heart softened. Her rock, Nik was. Passionate, idealistic like her, the yin to Athamos's rock-steady yang, she'd had to get to know him in pieces. He'd been sent off to join Athamos at boarding school when Stella was four, leaving her with only her nannies and tutor to keep her company while her mother immersed herself in her charity work as her marriage imploded.

She'd seen her brothers on holidays, had eagerly eaten up any time she'd had with them, missing them desperately when they left. When she'd gotten old enough to travel by herself, she'd visited Nik frequently in New York, hoping someday to join him there with her studies. But her parents had axed that dream.

She held his gaze now, as Constantinides electric blue as her own. *"S'agapao."* I love you. "You know that."

"Ki ego s'agapao." I love you, too. He enfolded her in a warm hug. "Now pick a dress. The party is days away."

Sofía and Alex returned with coffee and biscuits. Stella eyed the tray. "You think it's my blood sugar."

"We're working all angles," said Alex.

She smiled. Eyed the dresses. Felt her old fighting spirit rear its defiant head.

"I'm thinking the sapphire blue."

She was going to dazzle. She was going to shake things up. She was going to seize every ounce of her destiny and accomplish what she'd set out to do. The king had no idea of the storm headed his way.

Her storm surge was downgraded from a hurricane to a tropical storm by the time she made landfall at the Carnelian palace. Perched on a chain of mountains overlooking a vast green valley in one direction, with the Ionian Sea in the other, the cold and forbidding Marcariokastro was every inch the imposing medieval castle.

It conjured up the dark, suspenseful tales of her childhood, with its square ramparts, circular, capped turrets, moat and drawbridge, although the moat and drawbridge, it was to be noted, were no longer in use. Instead, a beautiful, pastoral lake surrounded the castle.

Stella had visited the massive, gray stone castle with her family years ago when relations between Akathinia and Carnelia had been peaceful; friendly, even. It had seemed a place of immense excitement and mystery to her then, its dungeon and weaponry rooms and long, stone labyrinth of hallways the perfect place for hide-and-seek.

She had always been the bravest of the kids, lasting the longest in her hiding spot, her goose bumps and chattering teeth nothing compared to the thrill of victory. Not even the brave Athamos had liked the dark. But settling into the spacious suite down the hall from the king's wing, where she would stay until she and Kostas were married, it suddenly felt more unnerving than exciting. Perhaps because the thought that this was now her home filled her with trepidation. Perhaps because she would miss Nik, Sofía and Alex terribly.

Immersed in meetings until late on the night of her

arrival, Kostas had left word he would see her the next morning. By the time he deigned to make an appearance as Page was doing Stella's hair for the party, the day had come and gone, the apprehension she hated herself for having once again kicking up a storm in her veins.

Nodding her head to Page to admit the king, she felt her stomach fill with a thousand butterflies. Clad in a bespoke, light gray suit and white shirt that emphasized his good looks, with his dark hair scraped back from his face, the sleek, powerful impact of him knocked her sideways.

She'd told herself she'd have her response to him firmly under control by now, but the spacious suite suddenly felt as if it had shrunk to the size of a shoe box when he strolled over to stand by her side at the dressing table, his gaze meeting hers in the mirror.

Moistening her lips, she searched for a smart remark but, for the life of her, couldn't think of one. His gaze slid to her mouth, as he appeared to absorb the evidence of her nerves, then dropped to the plunging neckline of her silk robe that had seemed respectable until he'd walked in, but now made her desperately want to pull the edges together.

She resisted the urge to do so. *Somehow.* The color riding his high cheekbones, the dark heat that claimed his whiskey-hued eyes as they lifted to hers, ignited a slow burn beneath her skin. Sparked a chemical reaction that climbed up into her throat and held her in its thrall.

He bent his head and brushed a kiss against her cheek. Unprepared, or perhaps *overprepared* for the press of his firm mouth against her sensitized skin, she flinched.

Kostas straightened, a dark glitter filling his eyes. Her gaze moved to Page, who was watching them with unabashed curiosity.

"Leave us," the king bit out quietly. Page scurried

from the room as if he'd been Zeus himself raising one of his thunderbolts.

Stella lifted her chin defiantly as the door closed and the room went silent. "You will need," he instructed tersely, "to learn to hide your very…*distinct* response to me when we're around others, when the cameras start flashing tonight, or this isn't going to be a very productive exercise."

Her chin lifted higher. "I don't *plan* it, Kostas. It just happens."

The glint in his eyes deepened. "Maybe we should do it again, then, maybe a *real* kiss this time, *practice*, so it doesn't happen tonight."

"I don't think that's necessary."

"Why not? Are you afraid of how you might respond?"

"Hardly." The pressure on her brain pushed her temper to its very edge. "But why stop there?" she challenged. "Why don't we *do* it right now? Up against the wall while Page is waiting… Would that *satisfy* you? Would that be enough of a *reaction* for you? To have the whole palace abuzz with how you keep me in line?"

He leaned his impressive bulk against the dresser, folding his arms across his chest. Dark amusement melted the ire in his eyes. "Is that the plan, Stella? To make me pay for entrapping you? To bait me until I fall over the edge? You forget how well I know you, how you deflect when you are stressed, when you feel *cornered*, how you use sarcasm as a weapon because that sharp mouth of yours is so very good at it."

She lifted a shoulder. "You have to work with the tools you're given."

His mouth curved. "Why don't you just tell me what's eating you?"

"Oh, what would be the fun of that? I'm enjoying

your amateur psychology course *so* much, I think *you* should tell *me*."

He pursed his lips. Eyed her. "It's been a trying two weeks. We've both been analyzed beyond endurance. Most of the Carnelians seem ready to welcome you, but some are reluctant to embrace a foreigner. Tonight is the night you must prove to them you belong. You wouldn't be human if you weren't feeling the pressure."

Remarkably spot-on. "I've been brought up in the media glare. I can handle it."

He inclined his head. "Regardless, I appreciate how you've risen to the occasion."

She had no smart comeback for that, so she left it alone. He flicked his gaze around the elaborately furnished, if exceedingly dark, suite. "How are you settling in?"

"Fine. Except honestly, Kostas, you were right. It's like you're caught in the Dark Ages here. Everything is cold, unforgiving stone. There's no warmth to the rooms, no *life*. How in the world do you live like this?"

"It's remained untouched since my mother died. My father refused to make changes. I agree, though, it needs massive renovations. It's hardly the kind of place I want to bring our children up."

There it was again. *Children. An heir.* She wished they could just forget about it for a while.

"What was it like?" she asked to distract herself. "Growing up here?"

"Lonely," he said matter-of-factly. "Cold. I've been told the life went out of the castle when my mother died. Some say that's when it left my father, too, and he became the dictator that he was."

"He loved her a great deal?"

"Too much, by all accounts."

Beauty and the Beast. She tipped her head to the side. "Was he really the man he was portrayed as?"

"A tyrant, you mean?" His mouth twisted. "It depended on which iteration of him you encountered. He was charming, charismatic and warm when he wanted to be, self-centered, compassionless and sadistic during his dark moods. A chameleon. A compulsive liar—to himself and others."

Sadistic. *Thee mou.* A chill went through her. "And to you, his son, what was he like?"

"I was his protégé from age five on. It was about learning the role, following in his footsteps. It was never a father-and-son relationship."

And what about the childhood, the *innocence,* he should have been allowed? She recalled a photo she'd seen in one of the hallways of the castle of Kostas and his father inspecting a military guard when the prince must have been just five or six, surrounded by hundreds of thousands of people. He had looked so lost...so bewildered.

The only man who could stand alone in the middle of a crowd. Kostas had been built that way, *conditioned* to stand alone, created by a man notorious for his lack of humanity. Her chest tightened. "Did he discipline you?"

"Beat me, you mean? Yes. It was part of his modus operandi. Fear and intimidation—the devices he used to control everyone around him. Sometimes it was physical, sometimes mental. He was a master at both."

"Please tell me you had someone, a grandmother, a *godmother,* someone you could go to?"

"My *yaya.* My grandmother on my father's side, Queen Cliantha. She died when I was twelve. But by then I was in school. It was an escape for me, a break from the brainwashing, the conditioning. I was lucky my father felt it necessary to present a civilized front to the world."

It may have been a break from the conditioning, but Kostas hadn't made many friends in school. By Athamos's account, he had always been the loner in the British boarding school they'd attended, the aloof presence that had been hard to get close to even though the Constantinides boys had tried to befriend him, having their own painful knowledge of a larger-than-life father.

Where had he drawn his strength? His belief in his vision? From some unshakable core inside of him?

She sank her teeth into her lip. "What happened when you developed a mind of your own? When it became apparent your philosophies differed from your father's?"

"I tried to keep them inside in the beginning. My grandmother said it was better that way. But eventually, as I gained in confidence, as I acquired external validation of my ideas, they came out. I was considered a threat then. A competitor. Anyone who questioned my father's practices was, and was suitably disposed of, but I, of course, posed the biggest threat of all—the blood heir who wanted a different way for his country. I wasn't so easy to contain."

"How could you coexist like that?"

"Uneasily. I made it clear to my father I would bide my time until it was my turn. In the meantime, I did the official engagements he couldn't manage, presented a civilized facade to the world, attempted to keep the internal workings of the country moving while he obsessed about taking Akathinia. But with the onset of his dementia, with his increasingly erratic behavior, it became harder and harder to talk sense into him—to stand back and do nothing."

Given how passionate Kostas had always been about

his beliefs, it must have been crippling for him. A gnawing feeling took root in her stomach. A feeling that she had been vastly unfair. "Things escalated before you left."

"Yes. There were those who wanted my father replaced, those who supported me and my democratic ideas and those who fought any decentralization of power that would strip them of theirs. It was a...tenuous situation threatening to implode at any minute."

With him squarely in the middle of it—loathe to turn on his own flesh and blood no matter how wrong his father's actions. Surrounded on all sides. The man in the middle of the storm.

The uneasy sensation in her gut intensified. She lifted her gaze to his. "Was that why you raced Athamos that night? Because you were frustrated? Because you weren't in your right head?

"It was...complicated."

Clearly, from the myriad of emotions consuming those dark eyes of his. The pieces of what had happened the night she'd lost her brother started to come together, beyond what Kostas had told her. She didn't like the doubt that invaded her head as they did. The gray zone it put her in with the man she needed to have zero feelings for.

Confused was not how she needed to enter this evening.

Kostas straightened away from the dresser. "I should get dressed." He handed her the sheaf of papers he was holding. "The final guest list. You should look it over."

She curled her fingers around the papers, glad for something to do rather than *feel* things for this man she shouldn't be feeling. "Anyone interesting coming out to play?"

"General Houlis and his two key lieutenants. You will stay away from them."

"Why?"

"Because they are dangerous men. You may think you are a dragon slayer, Stella, and no doubt you are, but this side of things you will not involve yourself in. Devote yourself to getting to know the people I've highlighted. They are key social, business and political figures who will be valuable to you."

She nodded. She would do that *and* get to know General Houlis, Kostas's biggest foe, because he would be her enemy, too.

Kostas headed for the door. Halfway there, he turned. "What are you wearing, by the way?"

"That will be a surprise."

His mouth tipped up at one corner. "I'm quite sure there will be enough of those tonight, but have it your way."

He left. Page returned to finish her hair. Stella immersed herself in the guest list, going over each key name and title, committing them to memory. Thank goodness hers was photographic.

When she'd made it to the *L*'s, her eyes widened. *Cassandra Liatos is attending?* The guest of Captain Mena, one of General Houlis's disciples, according to the list.

The woman Athamos had lost his life over. The woman her fiancé had most likely bedded.

Her pulse picked up into a steady thrum, blood pounding in her ears. *An unimportant detail Kostas had forgotten to mention?*

CHAPTER FOUR

"WE ARE *LATE*, Your Highness."

Kostas was well aware of that fact as he waited for Stella in the foyer of the castle, the arrival of their first guests imminent. The crowds, he had been told, were in the tens of thousands in the courtyard, all of them waiting for a glimpse of their king and future queen.

The global media was also impatiently waiting for them, three rows deep behind the red stanchions, cameras at the ready. The need to greet both the people and the media before their guests began arriving weighed heavily on his mind, along with the speech he was about to give, perhaps the most important of his career. He did not have time for a recalcitrant princess making yet another expression of protest.

A flash of blue caught his eye on the stairwell. As if her ears were burning, his future queen appeared. The hem of her ankle-length sapphire-blue gown in her hand, she made her way carefully down the steps. The look of focus on her face, the determined tilt of her chin, the fire that blazed in her electric-blue eyes, stopped his breath in his chest. She was out to conquer. He could read it in every stubborn line of her body…in the sheer force of will she was projecting. He'd never seen anything sexier in his life.

He drew in a deep breath so he could enjoy, *absorb*

the rest of the picture, for she was something to see. The gown that perfectly matched her incredible eyes wrapped itself around her slender curves in a seductive embrace that begged a man to do the same. Her hair, caught up in curls atop her head, revealed the long, slender sweep of her neck, the diamonds that glittered at her ears and throat reflecting the incandescent glow that blazed from inside of her, reaching out and wrapping itself around him.

Not for the first time in his life he found himself consumed by her. *Intrigued* by her. When Stella was in a room, everything else paled in comparison.

She stopped on the last step, eyes on his. Those sapphire-blue orbs widened imperceptivity as he made no effort to hide the effect she had on him—the way she owned him in that moment. The air between them was charged, heated. He left it like that, waiting to see what she would do. Mouth tightening, she lowered her chin, adopting that cool, blasé look he was beginning to recognize was her first line of defense.

"I'm sorry I'm late," she said crisply. "My hair was not right."

He studied the perfect curls. "There isn't a hair out of place."

"Now." She glanced toward the antique glass doors that led to the entrance of the castle. "There are thousands out there. I saw them from my window."

"Tens of thousands. And we are late. Are you ready?"

She nodded. He offered her his hand to help her down the last step. She took it, the fission of energy that passed between them as he wrapped his fingers around hers a living, breathing entity. Stella stared down at their clasped hands, then looked straight ahead as they walked to the doors.

He brought his mouth to her ear. "You look astonishingly beautiful. But where is the *back* of your dress?"

Her lips curved. "I thought we needed to shake things up a bit."

That she would do so had never been in question.

The flash of exploding camera bulbs was blinding as they stepped out onto the portico of the castle, a roar going up in the crowd that filled the courtyard. The electric excitement, the sense of anticipation that blanketed the night, sent a chill up his spine; brought his heart to a stuttering halt. The crowds assembled for his father had been coordinated, manufactured photo ops meant to send a message to the world of the power of his rule— the people paying lip service to the dictator for fear of reprisal should they not.

This was spontaneous. No one had been forced to come and yet…they had. Packed into the courtyard, the crowd spilled out onto the avenue beyond, confirming the rise in his approval ratings since the announcement of the coming elections and the news of his engagement to Stella. Proof that hope had taken root in his country.

A piece of him he had kept buried for months, *years*, a part of him that had survived the darkness, the self-doubt his father had instilled in him with every derisory remark about the fallibility of democracy, about his own inadequacies, throbbed in his chest. It was, he realized, his own hope. Somehow it had survived the hell he had endured.

If he continued to earn the people's trust, he could rebuild this nation. He could make everything that had been wrong *right*.

Stella squeezed his hand. He hadn't realized he'd stopped dead in his tracks. Looking down at her, their eyes held for a long, emotion-filled moment. *Go on*, hers seemed to say. *Seize the moment*.

They stepped forward and smiled and waved to the throng. The press was hungry for them, too. They gave them a photo before they took their place at the top of the stairs beside the Constantinides family as the first limousine rolled up.

A fully recovered, if fragile-looking, King Gregorios stood by Queen Amara, flanked by Nikandros, his wife, Sofía, Aleksandra and her husband, Aristos. That he was alone, yet again, struck him at the same moment as Stella's presence at his side filled that space inside of him. She was the strongest woman he knew.

Confident and utterly at ease, she greeted every guest with the perfect poise he had known she possessed, but it was her ability to connect with each one of the arrivals that blew him away. She found something in each brief greeting to make every encounter memorable, transforming like the chameleon she was—but it was always genuine. The skill was born of her royal heritage, yes, but it went deeper than that—to who she was, how she *cared*.

By the time they'd made their way through the first three flights of royalty, politicians and Carnelian high society deemed important enough for a personal greeting, he had had more than enough.

He pressed a hand to his fiancée's sexy bare back as the PR person gave the contingent the cue to go in.

Stella glanced at the crowd, who were still waving and calling their names. "We can't leave them like this."

"We need to. The agenda is tight."

She turned a vibrant blue beam of stubborn defiance on him. "If you want to *win* the people, Kostas, you have to *know* the people." And with that, she picked up her skirt and made her way toward the stairs.

He cursed under his breath and started after her. His bodyguard stepped forward. "You can't go into that crowd, Your Highness. You know the—"

"Threat," he said grimly. He was well aware he was a target for assassins. That there were many who would like to see him dead. But his future queen had now cleared the stairs and was accepting flowers from a young girl, the stubborn curve of her back *daring* him to follow.

He did. This time it was his bodyguard who cursed, rifled off a series of instructions to his security team, then followed him into the crowd. Stella gave him a sweet-as-pie smile as he made his way to her side, curving an arm around her waist. "This is ⌐ west coast. Your father once shook her hand.

He shook Berdina's hand. Then the hand of the elderly lady beside her that Stella had just finished hugging. *Hugging.* They worked their way through the front row, comprised of everything from those elderly ladies to children wishing to greet the royals to people anxious to confirm change was coming.

A man whose lined face had seen a great deal of life stepped forward and clasped his hands. "Will the elections really happen? We have waited so long for this."

"Yes," Kostas told him, "you have my word."

"But will they *mean* anything?" the man asked, doubt in his eyes.

"They will not be shadow appointments," he promised him. "The people will have real power. We are going to change this nation together."

By the time they were called back to the stairs by his frantic PR person, his throat felt as if it was lined with glass. He wrapped a firm hand around Stella's waist and directed her toward the stairs.

She aimed a satisfied look at him. "Glad you did it?"

"Yes," he said. "My security, however, is not."

"Why? Our bodyguards were with us."

"I am an assassination target, Stella."

Her mouth fell open. Staring at him, she missed her step and would have fallen had he not snared an arm around her waist and hauled her into him.

"Assassination target," she gasped. "Oh, my God, I didn't—"

"Think," he said, finishing her thought. "You were too busy making a point."

Her face went bright red.

"I know you're living to be a thorn in my side at the moment," he said as he directed her up the stairs and into the castle, "but could I please ask that you think before you act, particularly where protocol is concerned?"

Thee mou. Stella's head spun, blood pounding in her veins, as she matched Kostas's long strides through the doors of the castle and down the stone hallway toward the ballroom. She had not considered such a horrific thing and yet she should have. Kostas had detailed his enemies to her, outlined their hostility toward his rule. It only made sense he would be a target.

But *assassins*? Fear coated her mouth, gritty and dark. What she had been *trying* to do was shake Kostas out of that aloofness he protected himself with in a crowd. The stiff formality he had clearly learned from his father. She had felt his tension as soon as they'd emerged outside, and yet the emotion emanating from him had been anything but removed. He had been caught off guard by the people's response to him. By the joy they had displayed. Moved by it. He just didn't know how to show it.

"Lypamai," she murmured as they halted in front of the massive, gold-plated doors to the ballroom. *I'm sorry.*

Kostas looked down at her. "How about a little less wave-making and a little more obedience?"

Her jaw dropped. "As if I—"

He pressed a finger to her mouth, a brilliant smile lighting up his somber face. "I was just getting you going... You will need your fire in there tonight, *yineka mou*."

Her mouth burned where he touched her, the casual endearment throwing her completely off balance. She didn't want to feel this pulsing, inescapable connection to him that had burned between them ever since she'd walked down those stairs tonight. Ever since she'd first laid eyes on him.

As if he didn't look spectacular enough in full military dress, the severe black uniform adorned with gold buttons and a red sash playing up his hawk-like, brutal good looks. It made him appear larger than life—the weakness she'd always had for him.

She lowered her chin, the infinitesimal movement making him drop his fingers away from her mouth. "No need to worry about me. I've got this."

"That is the one thing I do not doubt."

A booming voice announced their arrival to the buzzing ballroom. She took Kostas's arm as they made their way through the crowd of almost five hundred guests toward the front of the room, where Nik stood waiting. The cacophony of sound as the guests applauded echoed off the hundreds of stained-glass windows that lined the room, highlighted to dramatic effect by the golden-hued arches that framed them.

The dark, seductive ambience lent by the stunning purple, gold and orange light from the glass windows highlighted by a dozen antique candelabra chandeliers scattered throughout the room seemed to set the tone for

the evening as she and Kostas took their place beside Nik
on a low balcony. Goose bumps unearthed themselves
on her skin as she took in the packed ballroom, a glittering, privileged crowd who would decide the king's fate.
Her fate, she corrected herself, for it was hers now, too.

Silence fell as Kostas greeted their guests. If he was
aloof in a crowd, he was compelling as an orator, his
even, measured tone underpinned by the passion he held
for his vision of a new Carnelia founded on the self-
determination of its people and the modernization of his
country to bring it into an "enlightened" age. If he knew
he was making enemies with some even as he attempted
to build trust with others, he was undeterred. He was
daring his people to accept his challenge, daring them
to dream of a brighter future.

"I'm ready to sign up," she murmured under her breath
as he finished and stepped back beside her to allow Nik
to take center stage.

He bent his head, his breath a warm caress at her ear.
"*Efharisto.* Perhaps in time you will be ready to sign on
to…*other* pieces of our partnership as things become illuminated."

She lifted her chin, cheeks burning. "In your dreams,
Kostas."

"You already are, Stella."

She kept her gaze averted from his, looked at the
crowd as Nik began speaking, refusing to engage. Except every part of her body *was* engaging with that seductive comment that had her excruciatingly aware of
him long after Nik had delivered an eloquent speech of
peace and friendship, and they had stepped off the balcony to mingle with their guests. It was not helped by
the firm hand Kostas kept at her bare back, his big paw
burning into her skin.

She hadn't thought about that aspect of the dress when she'd chosen it and really should have, because it made it difficult to concentrate on the important introductions being made with his splayed fingers declaring an ownership over her. A reminder of how strong and overwhelmingly male he was.

Firming her jaw, she forced herself to focus, attaching faces to the names Kostas had given her, familiarizing herself with each and every one of the VIPs as they engaged in polite, easy bites of small talk. She was laying the groundwork for relationships she would later build on, some of which would be a challenge she discovered because Carnelia seemed to be as closed an inner circle as Akathinia was. But others were open and curious, welcoming.

It was exhausting, the mental effort it took to absorb all that information about so many people, despite her razor-sharp memory. She was craving a break when Kostas stiffened by her side, his hand tightening around hers.

She followed his gaze to the couple directly in their path. The tall, dark-haired, middle-aged male wore a military uniform with enough stripes on the shoulder to indicate he was very senior. Not quite handsome, with his clearly defined, masculine features, but his piercing dark eyes held her attention. Her *yaya* had always said the eyes were the measure of a person and this man's dark stare held nothing good.

General Houlis.

Kostas drew her toward the couple, his hand at her waist. "General Houlis, I'm pleased to present my fiancée, Stella Constantinides. Stella, General Houlis is the commander of the Carnelian navy and a member of my executive council."

Stella held her hand out to the general, who took it

and bent lightly over it, the mocking significance of the gesture not lost on her. "A pleasure, Your Highness," he said, straightening. "Your presence here in Carnelia has been highly...*anticipated*."

The general made the introductions to his wife, then turned his attention back to Stella. "That was quite a reception for you two out there tonight."

She tilted her head. "It was wonderful. I am looking forward to restoring the close bonds Carnelia and Akathinia once shared. My childhood is full of those happy memories. It was also," she said deliberately, "lovely to see the excitement of the people about the forthcoming elections. Their belief a better future is ahead..."

"Indeed," said the general. "But are they ready for such widespread change? That is the real question."

"They've been ready for a long time now." Kostas set a deliberate gaze on the general. "Fear and intimidation have kept them silenced. Change is always hard, but for those who seek a better way, the short-term pain of the unknown will bring long-term gain. It is the faith we must all have. Those who resist change do so because it's in their own self-interest. They fear what they have to lose."

The general's eyes glittered. "Or they don't want the change that's being shoved down their throat. How many examples can we count of nations who've signed on to regional and global lovefests only to find the old ways were better?"

"Old ways as in the suppression of their rights? As in the fear for their own safety if they refuse to toe the line? I am sure you would agree that can hardly be called *better*."

"Sometimes," the general countered, "the people

aren't equipped to make such important decisions for themselves. Sometimes they don't have the vision required. It could all go to hell in a handbasket if not handled correctly."

"Which is why the transition time will be used to smooth the way." Kostas's tone was frigid now. "My belief in the Carnelian people is absolute. There is only one way forward for this country."

General Houlis lifted a shoulder. "Time will tell, won't it?"

Stella drew in a breath. The general turned to her. "You will certainly have a front-row seat to pursue your vision from your position on the executive council if the rumors are to be believed…"

She opened her mouth to respond. Kostas tightened his fingers around her waist. "We still have elections to carry out," the king said. "Many details to consider before the new council takes shape."

"But she will have a place on it?"

The disdain in the general's voice snapped her back straight.

"Her Highness," Kostas intoned, "will play a significant role in governing this country, yes."

"Don't you think," Stella interjected, "that it's time the council reflected a woman's perspective? The addition of some empathy, some *compassion*, to even out the testosterone-laden mistakes of the past? After all," she said, tilting her head to the side, "we aren't stuck in the Dark Ages anymore, are we?"

"No," said the general, "we aren't. It's when emotions get in the way of lawmaking that the mix gets murky."

Her gaze locked on his. "I *promise* you, General Houlis, my emotions will not obscure my clear thinking. I've found empathy, attempting to understand each other, *communicating*, has the power to solve some of the world's greatest conflicts. It can only be a powerful force when it comes to ruling a nation."

"And you bring a great deal of popularity with you to spread that message. Your work around the world has brought you much acclaim." He raised a brow. "The next Eva Perón, perhaps?"

"I would hardly make that comparison."

"Ah, but it's an intriguing one to consider. Some say that Eva, in fact, had all the power."

Kostas went dangerously still beside her. "Accumulating *power* is not the goal, General Houlis—putting it in the hands of the people is."

The other man lifted a shoulder. "I'm merely making the point that your future wife will be a force to be reckoned with."

A shiver went down her spine. Was there an underlying message there?

Kostas announced the need to move on. His hand at her elbow, he bid General Houlis and his wife farewell and propelled Stella through the crowd. He was practically vibrating with fury.

"When I *ask* you to refrain from adding fuel to the fire, you will do it. Your appointment to the council is a delicate move that requires much finessing. There is no point in making waves before the time comes."

"Perhaps you've changed your mind?"

He set his furious gaze on her. "I never go back on a promise—that you will learn, as well. But you need to be patient. We must take this in baby steps."

"I get that, Kostas, but I will not be *muzzled*. You will not tell me what I can and cannot say."

His gaze turned incendiary. "I may be giving you power, but I am still the king of this country, Stella. You *will* listen to me when I give you a direct order. *Obey* me when I ask for your cooperation."

Her skin stung as if he'd slapped her. "I have not agreed to the *obey* part yet. You might take that into consideration as you throw your weight around or you might find yourself minus a wife."

"Stella—"

"I need a break."

She shrugged her elbow free and stalked away, picking out Alex and Sofía in the crowd. Jaw clenched, she headed for them.

Alex eyed her as she approached. "What happened? You look positively combustible."

"Three guesses."

"Kostas, Kostas and Kostas." Her sister plucked a glass of champagne off a passing waiter's tray. "You clearly haven't had enough of this."

Clearly not. She took a sip of the bubbly. "I might kill him before this is over."

"What did he do now?"

"He told me I have to *obey* him."

Alex's mouth curved. "What did you say back?"

"That I haven't signed on to the *obey* part yet." She took a deep, calming breath. "How has your night been?"

Alex flicked a glance at Sofía. "Oh, *you know*, the usual chitchat. It's a bit disconcerting that these people were our enemies last year and now we're socializing with them."

"Not the people," Stella amended, "the leadership. And why do you have such a funny look on your face? What's going on?"

Alex directed another of those sideways looks at their sister-in-law. "Nothing, I—"

"Alex."

"Cassandra Liatos is here. The woman who—"

"I know who she is." Her heart thudded against her chest. "Where is she?"

"She's standing beside the chocolate fountain…with the man in the gray suit."

She turned in a subtle movement, locating the couple Alex had described. It must be Captain Mena in his sharply pressed military uniform standing beside Cassandra, but it was the woman herself who caught and held her attention. Of medium height, with the perfect, voluptuous figure she herself had always craved, Cassandra was astonishingly beautiful. As dark as Stella was fair, with long silky hair and exotic eyes, she was the kind of woman who stopped traffic.

The kind of woman men lost their heads over.

For a moment, she was unable to speak, unable to do anything but stare at the person who had turned her life upside down. "Does Nik know she's here?"

"Yes." It was Sofía who answered. "He elected not to speak to her."

She couldn't do it. She could not exercise that type of self-restraint. She didn't have it in her.

"I need to talk to her."

"I don't think that's a good idea." Alex put a hand on her arm. "Let it go, Stella."

But she was already walking toward the fountain. Cassandra looked up, eyes widening as she approached. Stella greeted Captain Mena first, then the woman at his side. "May I have a moment of your time?"

The other woman nodded, the tempest in her dark eyes the only sign that this was anything other than a polite social interaction. Stella led the way out of the ballroom and onto one of the outdoor terraces. Face-to-face with the woman who had dogged her thoughts for weeks, she took a deep breath.

"Efharisto," she murmured. "I'm sorry to pull you away."

Cassandra shook her head. "When I saw Nikandros, I wanted to speak to him. My fiancé persuaded me not to. He said it was better left alone."

"Everyone seems to think that." Stella wrapped her arms around herself, resting her champagne glass against her chest. "I need to know if you loved my brother. If he loved you. It's the only rational explanation I can find for him to do something so out of character. Yes, the competition between him and Kostas has always been the height of stupidity, but it had to have been more."

Cassandra put her glass on the railing, taking a moment, as if to gather her thoughts. "I cared about both of them," she said, lifting her gaze to Stella's. "You need to know that. I felt as if I was in an impossible situation. I knew the history behind them. It made it very…difficult."

"But you must have had stronger feelings for one than the other?"

"I was in love with Kostas," Cassandra said quietly. "I adored Athamos, but it was Kostas I wanted."

She was unprepared for the sharp claws of jealousy that climbed inside her and dug deep into her soft recesses. For the jagged pain that raked itself over top of it on behalf of her brother's ill-fated gamble. Athamos had not loved easily, as had been the case with all her siblings after her parents' disastrous example of a marriage, but when he'd fallen, he'd fallen hard.

"Did he know?"

"I don't know. I told them both I needed time to think. I was trying to work out how to tell Athamos it wasn't him I wanted. It was—" Cassandra pressed her hands to her cheeks. "It was done before I even knew what was happening. The first thing I knew of it was when I opened the newspaper the next day and saw the news of the crash."

When Athamos was dead. "Do you wonder," she asked, unable to stop herself, "if you'd said something sooner...?"

Cassandra paled, her deep olive skin assuming a gray cast. "Every day. Every day since it happened. But at some point I had to forgive myself. Move on. Punishing myself wasn't going to bring Athamos back. It wasn't going to change what happened."

Stella bit hard into her lip, the metallic taste of blood filling her mouth. She should tell Cassandra it wasn't her fault, that she couldn't have predicted what would have happened, but a tiny part of her couldn't forgive the woman for not sharing the truth with Athamos before things got out of hand. And because she suspected Cassandra had been hedging her bets. If the crown prince of Carnelia had fallen through as a potential mate, she could have picked up the pieces with Athamos and still become queen.

She studied the woman across from her. "Have you found happiness now, with your fiancé?"

Cassandra's gaze dropped away from hers, but not before she caught the myriad of emotion that ran through those dark eyes. *The sadness.* "I have found...peace."

"With a man who wants to take the potential for that away from this country?"

The other woman lifted her chin. "It isn't wise to judge others until you've walked in their shoes."

But the deep, searing flare of jealousy invading Stella didn't care about fairness. Athamos was dead. Cassandra Liatos was still clearly in love with Kostas. Perhaps their relationship, made impossible according to her fiancé, had never really finished. Perhaps Kostas still loved her. It made her feel ill in a way she'd never experienced before.

And that, she told herself, was ridiculous. Her and Kostas's marriage was not a love match. It was a partnership. It was, however, a potent reminder of what it would cost her to allow her old feelings for her fiancé to resurface. To allow them to rule her.

She lifted her gaze to Cassandra's. "I wish you and Captain Mena the best of luck. I hope you find the peace you are looking for. I really do."

Turning on her heel, she strode inside. Alex had been right. That had been no kind of closure.

"How many High Court justices will you appoint?"

Kostas attempted to concentrate on his conversation with a high-ranking Carnelian judge, but the sight of his fiancée in the arms of Aristos Nicolades had unearthed a strange, combustible force inside of him that felt a great deal like jealousy. A foreign emotion he had little experience with. If he wanted a woman, he pursued her and enjoyed her. If she played games, one of those ineffectual exercises designed to inspire him to think seriously about her, she was gone within the hour.

But right now, watching Stella enclosed in the casino magnate's arms on the dance floor, an intense conversation going on between the two of them, he was not unaffected. He wanted to walk over there and end it.

Exhaling a long breath, he pushed his attention back to the woman in front of him, a powerful figure who was a key supporter and would be an ally in the justice system. "I'm not sure yet. Rest assured, you will be among them."

He concluded his conversation with the judge, making his way toward the dance floor, attempting to corral his temper while he was at it. It was tradition that the engaged couple kicked off the dancing, but since his fiancée had been out on the terrace with Cassandra Liatos, a collision he hadn't been able to prevent, then taken to the dance floor with Aristos, he'd had to cool his heels while his event planner continued to look as if she might burst a blood vessel.

He was also feeling as if he might burst a blood vessel at his fiancée's latest rebellion. He caught her hand as she walked off the dance floor with Aristos and the look of careless disregard on her face sent his blood pressure up another ten points.

"That line I was talking about earlier," he murmured in her ear as he directed her to the side of the dance floor. "We're fast approaching it."

She turned near violet eyes on him. "What happens when we do? Will you *discipline* me?"

"The thought is vastly appealing."

Her eyes widened. "You wouldn't lay a hand on me."

"No, I wouldn't. Not in anger. There are many forms of discipline, *yineka mou*. I would find an appropriate one for you."

A layer of heat stained her perfect skin. Dropping her chin, she leveled a heated glance at him. "You *knew* she would be here and you didn't tell me."

"Cassandra?"

"Yes."

"She was on the guest list. I knew you'd see it. I didn't see the point in rehashing the whole subject again."

"Rehashing it?" She stared at him. "My brother died when that car plunged off the cliffs. Excuse me for wanting the whole story."

"I've apologized. I've told you the story, Stella. It needs to be finished."

She set her hands on her hips. "Were you afraid I would discover she's still in love with you? Are *you* still in love with *her*, Kostas? I'd like to know the lay of the land before I walk into this marriage. Will there be three of us in it?"

"No," he said flatly. "I am not in love with her. I told you it ended at the time. But I am happy to see you care. Maybe there's hope for us yet."

"I don't *care*," she growled. "I am more concerned with being humiliated."

But she did. He could see it in the green-eyed jealousy consuming her. It filled him with a supreme sense of satisfaction as the bandleader gave them the signal to take to the dance floor. Wrapping his fingers around hers, he led her to the center of the space that had been cleared for them. "Perhaps you should concern yourself instead with the fact that it is Carnelian tradition that we kiss during the first dance, and since everyone will be waiting for it, we'd better do a convincing job."

Her eyes flew to his as he curved an arm around her waist and laced his fingers through hers to pull her close. "Why didn't you tell me about this?"

"Ask yourself that, *paidi mou*, and I'm sure you'll come up with the answer."

Her skin paled. "Stop using those ridiculous endearments. They hardly suit us."

"I beg to differ." He directed her through the first steps of the dance. "I think they are perfect."

She was stiff, but there was undeniable fire beneath his fingers. He could feel the pulse of her fury, sense the scattered direction of her thoughts as she looked for a way out of the inevitability to come.

"Perhaps you should just enjoy it."

"Perhaps I should close my eyes and channel a former lover. Think about someone I actually *want* to kiss. It would provide far more inspiration than the thought of kissing you."

Heat flared under his skin, jealousy rocking him hard. A tight smile twisted his lips as he closed his fingers around hers and drew her closer. "Refuse me, Stella, deny how you feel, but don't ever, *ever*, tell me lies."

Fury drove him as he clasped his fingers around her jaw and brought his mouth down on hers in a kiss that stamped his possession all over her. That made it clear to anyone in the room, to *her*, that he was the only one who would touch her this way. To expose her lies for what they were.

Stiff at first, she yielded only enough to cover up the animosity swirling between them. But then the kiss morphed, changed into something entirely different. Her soft, tempting mouth beneath his threw him back ten years to another kiss, another time, when her belief in him had been a shining light in the darkness that had consumed him. Reminded him who she was. The woman who had stood on those stairs outside with him tonight and prompted him to seize the moment. The woman who had agreed to take a massive leap with him with the ending yet unknown.

Gentling the kiss, he exercised a more persuasive possession. His thumb at her jaw stroked its way across her satiny skin, his hand at her waist drew her into the heat they generated. A tiny, animalistic sound emerged from her throat as he angled his mouth across hers, lips sliding over lush, sacred territory, caressing her with a reverential touch that demonstrated her potent effect on him.

A sigh left her lips as she gave in, mouth softening,

parting for him. He claimed her then with a kiss that was pure in its origins, both of them giving of themselves without reservation, hot and sweet all at the same time. A shudder went through her, vibrating its way along his nerve endings. It caught him off guard. Tapped something deep and latent in him, claimed *him* in a way he hadn't expected.

For a brief moment in time, oblivious to the hundreds of people in the room, the truth existed between them. That this...*this* had always been right.

CHAPTER FIVE

STELLA BLINKED AS Kostas lifted his head from hers, the blinding spotlights on the dance floor flickering in her eyes as she attempted to focus. Her palms were damp, her knees weak, and her heart thrummed in her chest as the undeniable affects of his kiss reverberated through her.

That had been a full-on, five-star Robert Doisneau kiss right there, rolled up in some Mary Poppins magic. The kind she couldn't have fought no matter how hard she'd tried, because this was Kostas delivering it, the man whose kiss she'd measured all others against. Jessie had been right about that.

Her fluttering heart plummeted to the toes of her Christian Louboutin shoes. She'd been fooling herself all these years hoping she could find that magic with someone else because it had only ever been Kostas who could inspire it.

The stomach-churning realization settled over her as she unlocked her gaze from the man throwing her into confusion and attempted to wrestle her composure back as catcalls and applause broke out around them.

"Pulling out the big guns, Kostas?"

"If I was pulling out the big *guns*, we certainly wouldn't be standing on the dance floor," he returned with a velvety soft composure that made her crazy. "I'll save that for when you finally admit how you feel."

She had no smart comeback for that because she was quite sure her feelings were still plastered across her face. She focused on Nik and Sofía instead. They had joined them on the dance floor, along with a dozen other couples. She moved her gaze elsewhere when her brother's amused expression sent another wave of heat to her cheeks.

She and Kostas had been dancing the night of her mother's birthday party all those years ago, the night she'd made her big mistake with him. Her dream of becoming a lawyer in tatters, the fury and frustration she'd been trying to hold in all night overcoming her, and Kostas had seemed to be the only one to recognize her misery.

He'd pulled her off the dance floor and out to the library so she could collect herself. Except alone in the library, their attraction toward each other had caught fire after a summer spent dancing around it. Kostas had just arrived home, fresh from flight school in California with Athamos, taking his place as a captain in the Carnelian navy, a *man* when all the others had been boys. A man with an edge that turned her heart and hormones upside down.

Even among all the female adulation he'd engendered with his aloof, unattainable air, he'd always made time for her. Had always *listened* to her. When he'd kissed her in the library, she'd been sure she'd met her soul mate. Everything in her miserable, lonely existence had felt better, the pain of having her self-determination stripped away replaced by the heart-pounding excitement of being in Kostas's arms.

For a brief moment in that painful adolescence, she

had felt whole, as if she hadn't been missing some crucial piece that made her so unlovable. So defective she could never seem to do anything right. She'd waited for Kostas in his bed, thinking he'd be thrilled to find her there after the kiss they'd shared that had felt like a revelation. Instead, he'd shattered her heart with the callous, mortifying dismissal he'd administered.

Her eyelids squeezing closed, she banished the memory to the recycle bin of her mind and this time she *would* empty it. She was no longer that hopelessly naive, vulnerable girl looking for a fairy tale that didn't exist. For a man who didn't exist. So Kostas had caught her off guard with that kiss… She just needed to try harder to channel the impenetrability she aspired to.

Her emotions too close to the surface, she stayed silent during the rest of the dance. Completed the remainder of her obligatory turns around the spotlighted floor in the same self-protective state until it was finally time to wish their guests farewell.

She stood by Kostas on the front steps of the castle and waved everyone off as the early hours ticked by on the clock. After a nightcap with Nik, Sofía, Alex, Aristos and her fiancé in the Gothic-inspired conservatory, she went to bed. Except as tired as she was, she kept staring at the ceiling of the creepy, dark room.

So it turned out the remnants of her old crush were actually a dangerous adult attraction toward a man she was realizing she may have vastly misjudged, a far more dangerous proposition than the first. Her defense strategy for this marriage remained the same. She needed to take her attraction to Kostas and banish it to the deep, dark place she harbored inside her for the heartbreak she'd accumulated more than her fair share of.

Kissing him in public had been an unforeseen, necessary diversion from the master plan. She wouldn't have to do it again until their wedding day and that was four whole weeks away. Lots of time to render herself immune to the king.

The week that followed saw both Stella and Kostas wrapped up in their own separate endeavors. Kostas worked insane hours planning the elections and meeting with foreign investors as he attempted to jump-start Carnelia's economy with an aggressive modernization plan, while Stella followed up with the contacts she'd made at the engagement party, booking meetings with various charities and organizations she wanted to get involved with.

She wanted to dig in, to discover the issues Carnelians faced after decades of King Idas's totalitarian rule. What she found was disheartening. The people were suffering both emotionally and economically, leaving them bruised and battered, cynical and distrustful. It was going to take a great deal of time and hard work to heal them and put this country back together.

On Friday, she returned home from a meeting with the head of the largest social services charity to find Kostas walking in the door at the same time. Powerful and compelling in a dark navy suit and red tie, the lines bracketing his eyes and mouth revealed the pressure he was under to repair this broken country with so many opposing forces in play. The dark, intense aura somehow managed to make him even more dangerously attractive.

They'd been like two ships passing in the night, but when they did manage to sit down together for a quick meal there was an ever-present and unresolved tension between them. Neither of them had forgotten that kiss. They were simply choosing to avoid it.

"Long day?" She attempted a polite, even interaction.

He set down his briefcase, raked a hand through his thick, dark hair and focused his tawny gaze on her. "Exceedingly long. I thought I'd unearth a bottle of good burgundy from the cellar, since we're staying in tonight. We can sit down to a civilized dinner for once. A date if you like."

Her nerve endings tingled. "Aren't we a bit past that?"

His catlike eyes hardened. "We are getting married in three weeks, Stella. We need to spend some time together, learn how to interact, get to know each other better. So no, I don't think we're past it. I think it's perfect timing."

The rebuke rippled across her skin. "All right," she said, lifting a hand to slide her bag off her shoulder. "I will go and get changed. A power suit puts me in a particular frame of mind."

An amused glint entered his gaze. "So what will you change into, *yineka mou*? Your agreeable, soft, feminine side? If so, I'm all for it."

"I'm not sure I have that."

"Oh, you do, Stella." His sleek, sensual rejoinder slid down her spine like silk. "All it takes is the right mood to bring it out."

With that kiss that had brought her to her knees far too fresh in her mind still, she cocked her chin at a defiant angle. "Is that your specialty, Kostas, with all those women you collected? Wining and dining them so you unearthed their *soft, agreeable sides*?"

He lifted a shoulder. "Sometimes it required dinner, sometimes not. But since you are my fiancée, your presence at dinner is *my* pleasure."

Thee mou, but he was arrogant. It didn't stop her head from going to that story Athamos had told her—of Kostas setting his attention on a particular woman in a bar near the base where they'd trained at Miramar. The rumor went that he'd had her outside against the back of the bar—no dinner needed there. The woman, according to Athamos, had returned to the bar with a very satisfied look on her face.

"Stella?"

She blinked. "Sorry?"

"I'll meet you in the dining room."

Mouth tight, she climbed the stairs to her room. Deliberately picking out the furthest thing from what could be considered sexy attire, she dressed in black leggings and a loose-fitting, gypsy-style blouse she loved. Kostas's gaggle of women might have been easy targets, but she was *not*.

Kostas registered Stella's reappearance with amusement. If she thought the outfit she had on less than *agreeable*, she was mistaken. The leggings emphasized the long sweep of her elegant legs to perfection, providing a tantalizing glimpse of firm, toned thighs and smooth hips, just enough to fill a man's hands. The turquoise blouse, while covering her fully, was sheer enough to hint at the delectable curves beneath.

Blood headed south fast, something that hadn't happened since before he'd left for Tibet. In his quest to find himself, his guru had preached abstinence as the path to clarity. Having had no desire to have a woman, it had been an easy practice to follow. But not now. Not with his sexy fiancée baiting him at every turn.

Right now, with the frustration and tension of the day throbbing through him, finding an empty room, backing her up against a wall, wrapping Stella's beautiful legs around his waist and solving this friction between them exactly as she'd suggested that night in her suite held great appeal. *Hot, hard and fast.*

Unfortunately, he conceded, as he picked up his fiancée's wineglass and filled it as she sat down beside him, he couldn't do that. Ensuring his fiancée thawed enough to make this partnership of theirs a viable proposition was his goal tonight. Figuring out what had made her so cynical, so *brittle*, was a big part of that. Hot sex was not.

"So," he said as she gave him a wary look, "tell me about your day."

She took a sip of her wine. Cradled the glass in her palms. "Almost all of the RSVPs for the wedding are in. I'm shocked at how many can make it, almost three-quarters of those we invited."

"They are curious. Curious to see if this Camelot they have invoked is the real thing."

Her mouth twisted in that sexy, slightly crooked smile that had always fascinated him. *Turned him on.* "Now to live up to such an ideal."

"Not possible—that's why it's a myth."

She lifted a shoulder. "This afternoon I met with Theda Demarchis. She offered to give me a tour of the various charities her organization runs. We saw two of them this afternoon."

"The system is not in good shape, I know. My father drove the country into the ground before he died. Used far too much of the public funds to tighten the reins on the people, for his security, rather than to help them prosper. I've been returning what I can to organizations like Theda's, but the funds we receive from the foreign investment will be the real key."

Her mouth pursed. "It was sad, to see how this once proud country has diminished. There are so many who need help, so many who have suffered so greatly."

A knot formed in his gut. At his failure to stop his father. At allowing it to get this far. "It is painful to see," he agreed. "But slowly it will get better. The foreign investment, the hotel developments, will also create jobs. Unemployment is a big problem."

"Speaking of which." She pressed her wineglass to her chin. "I had a cappuccino in town after my meeting. The proprietor of the café sat down at my table, worried the hotels are going to obstruct his view and take away business."

He shrugged. "They might. This isn't about one store owner's view, it's about revitalizing the nation's economy."

"Yes, but he isn't *just* one person. He's an influential voice in the community. He sees the townspeople every day, talks to them, tells them what he thinks."

"So what did *you* tell him?"

"That more tourists means more business for him."

"Exactly how he needs to view it." He shook his head. "I think, somehow, the people are looking for roses and sunshine from me, when what they really need is actual solutions to their problems."

She frowned. "Three generations of that man's family have run that café, Kostas. It's the best view in town. I'm not saying there easy answers, I'm not saying change is going to come easily for people or that you can accommodate all of their requests, but perhaps you can accommodate some. In this instance, perhaps, keep the buildings low-rise like we have in Akathinia." She lifted her glass to her lips and took a sip. "I told him to write you a letter."

"A *letter*?"

"Yes. And you will answer it. You saw the night of our engagement party how much distrust and cynicism exists among the people. The only way you are going to win your people back is to show them the empathy and care your father never did. Prove to them they can trust you."

His mouth flattened. "They also need to trust *me*. Let me do my job. If I get mired down in what every café owner thinks, I'll never get anything accomplished."

She shook her head. "You need to choose your key influencers carefully. Those closest to the people. That café owner is one of them. You need to listen to him."

Stella watched Kostas over the rim of her wineglass as the salad was served. She was pushing him, but he needed it. His default mode was to know everything, to fix Carnelia's problems the most efficient way he knew, but that wasn't going to work here. He couldn't be a one-man show.

However, a man like Kostas, so utterly sure in his opinions, needed to find his own way to the truth.

They managed to pass the meal in a distinctly civilized fashion. By the time it was through, the excellent wine and the chance to relax had her feeling distinctly mellow.

Kostas picked up the bottle of wine. "Let's finish it in the conservatory."

She followed him there. He sprawled out on the small sofa, long legs splayed in front of him. She headed for one of the wing-backed chairs beside it.

"Sit here." His command pulled her to a halt. She turned to look at him. "You may have decided our intimate relationship will be conducted on an as-needed basis," he drawled softly, "but that doesn't mean you have to sit a mile away."

The glimmer of challenge in his dark perusal was too much to resist. Curling up on the other end of the sofa, she discovered she had little room, as his big frame hogged the space and a hard thigh pressed against hers.

She pulled in a breath only to find *him* in her lungs. Spicy aftershave with a rich, dark undertone that was all Kostas, pure carnal male.

She handed him her glass to refill. The brush of his fingers against hers transferred his masculine heat, amplifying her awareness of him.

Seriously, Stella. She searched for an innocuous subject. "I had the interior designer come by this morning. I can't live in this mausoleum one minute longer. He's going to have some plans to us next week."

"Good." He handed the glass back to her. "Can he start in the master suite? Perhaps he could have it finished by the wedding?"

When she would move in there with him, *share his bed*, sometimes in an intimate fashion. Her stomach curled in on itself. "Might be possible." She chewed on her lip. "He was wondering about a nursery. Do we want it connected to our suite?"

"Yes. I want our children to be close in case they have a nightmare or they need us."

Children—plural. She swallowed. "How many children are you planning for us to have?"

"More than one. Maybe three? Four?"

"Four?" That would require much *baby-making*, particularly if it didn't happen right away.

His mouth kicked up at one corner. "I want lots of kids, Stella. And not because I want to turn you into a *broodmare*. Because I never had siblings...because I never want our children to feel the isolation I once did."

A vise closed around her chest. She couldn't get his pain out of her head—the childhood he'd led, how destructive it must have been to his soul... It had haunted her as she'd stared at the damn creepy shadows at night trying to sleep.

"How did you cope?" she asked huskily. "I keep thinking about you by yourself. You were only twelve when your grandmother died. How did the world even make sense?"

He cradled his glass against his chest. "I retreated into myself. I lived in my own little world. My grandmother kept pulling me out, engaging me, forcing me to find a sense of self. She knew I would need that strength when she was gone."

She wrapped her arms around herself and hugged tight. "She was a popular queen from what I remember."

"Both her and my grandfather, King Pelias, were very popular, benevolent monarchs of the people—not the ambitious, controlling rulers of the past. Unfortunately, my grandfather's ill health took him very young and my father became king perhaps sooner than he should have. It was up to my grandmother to guide my father then, but after my mother died, he became unreachable. She began coaching me instead. Every night when I went to visit her, she taught me the principles of what she believed in, what being a good ruler meant—that they were *of* the people, not *over* the people."

"And what you learned at school, during your time in the West, the philosophies you developed, were grounded in what she had taught you."

"Yes."

She pressed her palms to her cheeks, remembering the loneliness she'd felt. Imagining it ten times worse because there would also be *fear*. Her gaze rested on him; so stoic, resolute, like he *always* was. "It was so much for a child to absorb. To *understand*."

A hint of emotion flickered in his dark eyes. "She told me whenever I lost my way, when I harbored doubts about which direction to go, to always remember to be a force of good. That I would be afforded great power, but with that came the responsibility to use it wisely. That if I was strong and followed my heart, I would not fail."

A wave of emotion swept over her, tightening her throat, spurring a wet heat at the back of her eyes. To be so brave, to carry his grandmother's wisdom with him throughout his life and somehow manage not to be consumed by the force his father had been, struck her as remarkable. *Extraordinary.* But it also illuminated her own shortcomings. Whereas Kostas had been defined by his duty, she had spurned hers, acting out in her need to have someone acknowledge the pain and isolation she had felt. But that acknowledgment had never come—not from the place she'd needed it most.

His dark lashes lowered. "Your childhood was also difficult. You never said much, but I could see how painful it was for you. Athamos and Nik were better at hiding it."

She lifted a shoulder. "You know what my father is like. He doesn't have it in him to love anyone. My mother was too broken by his affairs to want to be anywhere near us. I was raised instead by three very conscientious nannies who tried to hide the fact that they felt very, very sorry for me. And even they didn't last long because of the toxic atmosphere."

"It could not have been easy for you to watch your mother go through that. To see your family torn apart."

All the while in the glare of the media spotlight. Never a moment of escape… "My life was supposed to be perfect," she said, a brittle edge to her voice. "To everyone else it was perfect—to me it was hell. My mother was a tragic figure stripped of her self-worth and pride, forced to carry on a facade. I, in turn, was supposed to act the fairy-tale princess, living my fairy-tale life, when in reality it was anything but."

He took a sip of his wine, his intense scrutiny remaining on her. "Instead, you rebelled. You skipped out on boarding school, you partied, you dated all the wrong men…"

She narrowed her gaze. "Is that a statement or a question?"

"I'm simply trying to understand you, Stella. The woman you've become. Just like you just were with me."

"I'm not that rebel anymore."

"But it goes to what shaped you. I'm curious, though, about where all the cynicism is coming from…about what you said in Barbados—that relationships *just aren't worth it.*"

"Life," she said flatly. "That's where it's coming from. Life."

He lifted a brow.

"And what were all the men about? Choosing the most unavailable ones who'd never commit so you'd never know the hurt your mother did?"

She blinked. "Which men are you referring to?"

"The captain of the English national football squad—the most notorious womanizer in Europe—the South African mining magnate with his third divorce behind him, the American rancher with two women on the go…"

She could tell by his face he thought she'd slept with them all. That he believed the tabloids when, in fact, most of them had been lies. It made her blood heat. *He*, of all people, should know better.

She lifted her chin. "What's wrong with having some fun? You have surely had your share. You're the poster child of no-strings-attached, meaningless relationships."

JENNIFER HAYWARD 85

"I am not you. You wanted more. You told me you wanted more. What happened to the Stella I knew?"

Her blood fizzled hotter. "What do you want to know about them, Kostas? Why I was with them? Why I slept with them?" She put her fingers to her mouth. "Well, let's see, I gave my virginity to Tony Morris after you turned me down. It was after his big game in Prague and can I tell you what a long, hot ride that was? Maybe I should be thanking you for that one. Then I dated Angelo Adamidis, whose ego was even bigger than Tony's, which didn't really appeal to me, followed by—"

"Stamata." He put his wineglass down, liquid sloshing up the sides. "That's enough."

"What's the matter?" She directed a defiant look at him, heart pounding at his flared nostrils, the sizzling heat in those whiskey-colored eyes. "You *asked* for the details… Does it *antagonize* you to hear that about your future wife? Or perhaps you're miffed because you missed out? That you misjudged me… That all I wanted was a hot roll between the sheets and some other male enjoyed the privilege?"

A silence passed, so long, so extended, she had to fight the urge not to fidget, to look away from the intensity of his laser-like expression as it branded her skin. "If I'd known all along that was what you were after," he finally said quietly, "I would have taken you up on your offer. But I don't think that's what it was, was it?"

Her gaze fell away from his. Her initiation into sex with Tony had been awful, his ego rendering him utterly insensitive to a woman's pleasure. She had stumbled away from that horrific experience vowing never to do it again and almost hadn't. There had always been something missing for her in the sexual act—an emotional bond, something beyond the physical.

She lifted a shoulder, deflecting the need to go more than surface-deep because that was where she liked to stay these days. "What does it matter?"

"It matters. Look at me, Stella."

She did, then wished she hadn't because he saw right through her. Always had.

"That kiss," he stated, "was the truth of us. You know it and I know it. You vibrate every time we're within ten feet of each other, yet you refuse to admit it. You fight me at every turn because you don't know how to handle this thing we have. But at some point it's going to have to stop. You are going to need to learn that I am not your father. I will not hurt you like he hurt your mother. I am the man who has always respected you enough to treat you the way you deserve."

She caught her bottom lip between her teeth, fighting for impassivity. "So now that I've agreed to become your wife, now that you're about to bestow upon me the lauded title of Mrs. Kostas Laskos, I should fall into your bed and count my lucky stars I'm the *chosen* one? I don't think so, Kostas. I've given you the agreed-upon parameters of this relationship. That's how it's going to work."

"I'm not disputing that. What needs to end is this standoff, this mistrust you have of me, the tension between us. We need to have a *relationship* if this partnership is going to work."

She considered him over her glass. "What exactly is it you're suggesting? Sex as intimacy? A mutual understanding based on our pheromones so we can produce that heir you need? Because the last time I checked, you were still the most emotionally unavailable man I know, Kostas. That little boy you talked about? He grew up into a big, life-size version of himself. You let people in so far, then you shut them down."

His olive skin stretched taut across his aristocratic face. "We will have to find a way to work through our failings. There is no other option."

Because his children were a task he had to tick off his list, as was *she*. He would fix his personal life as he was fixing the legacy that had been left on his doorstep. All he knew was to eye the end goal and attack the obstacles in between.

She set her jaw. "We'll make this work. We both have too much at stake for any other outcome. As for the rest, the *trust*, it's earned. You can't snap your fingers and order it to be so."

The glitter in his eyes said he thought he could. "We have a mutual respect for each other, we *appreciate* one other. We can have something good, we can be different than the relationships we've experienced in the past, if you will stop throwing every advance I make in my face."

She put down her wineglass. The wine was making her head too hazy, too *unclear*. She needed to put some distance between herself and this man who stirred far too much emotion in her, who liked to push every wish of his through like a steamroller, running over everything in between.

She knew they couldn't sustain this tension between them. Knew they had to make this work. But investing herself in something with Kostas that was halfway between hate and love—the gray area he was asking for? Was that even possible while keeping her emotions under wraps?

"I need some sleep."

"I have more work to do. I'll walk you up."

She thought that was a bad idea, but she couldn't refuse given his study was down the hall from her room. Silently she climbed the massive staircase beside him to the third floor, where the royal wing was located. Defenses not as solid as they should be, she crossed her arms over her chest and stared up at him as they stopped outside her bedroom door.

"Thank you for dinner."

His mouth twisted. "We almost remained civilized."

Almost being the operative word. She wasn't sure she and Kostas were ever going to get to civilized.

He bent toward her, his delicious, dark scent invading her senses. Heart hammering in her chest, she froze, debating whether to accept or reject his kiss. His mouth landed on her cheek instead. Firm and undeniably male, his lips made a slow, sensual journey up to her ear, her skin firing beneath his touch.

"*Kalinihxta*, Stella." His low voice raked across her insides. "Sweet dreams."

Straightening away from her, he walked toward his study. She let herself into her suite and leaned back against the door, her insides a mass of confusion.

Only Kostas could ever make her shake over a *non-*kiss.

Kostas worked for another couple of hours, then gave up, his head too cloudy to accomplish anything. In the master suite, dominated by the dark colors and fabrics Stella hated, but which had great bones with its exposed stone walls, he stripped off his clothes and immersed himself in the steam shower, one of the few modern amenities his father had added in deference to his bad lower back.

Sitting down on the bench, he let the water pour over him and eat away at the tension bunching his muscles. Negotiating foreign investment with a dozen different countries, spearheading the country's first elections and dealing with a recalcitrant executive council seemed like child's play compared to understanding the woman Stella had become. She wasn't the innocent, vulnerable girl he'd once known, wasn't the rebel she'd spent years as, but was something else entirely.

Philanthropist, cynic, hardened veteran of life at twenty-seven. Moving out of the hot, hard spray, he sat back against the tile, sluicing the water out of his face. He'd always known Stella's life had scarred her badly, but tonight he'd gotten a glimpse at how wounded she really was.

Closing his eyes, he recalled their conversation. *Trust is earned.* His fiancée's rebuttal to his request they develop some sort of manageable, doable relationship between them. He would do it, had to do it, but Stella was right—his ability to be in a relationship, to be emotionally available, had always been in question.

He had been conditioned to never show emotion, never feel it, or allow himself that luxury. Designed to be impenetrable. Other than his grandmother's affection, he'd never had love, didn't know what it was, nor did he want it. Maybe it had been watching his father fall down a rabbit hole when his mother had died, one from which he hadn't emerged whole. He just knew it wasn't for him, wouldn't ever be.

Which, he thought, wiping a layer of perspiration from his brow, shouldn't be an issue given Stella's pronouncement she wasn't interested in love, wanted to make herself as impenetrable as he was. It was just that he wasn't sure she had meant it, wasn't sure a lot of the Stella he'd seen today wasn't just tough packaging over the real thing and that woman *was* exceedingly vulnerable, had always wanted more.

And therein lay the problem. He couldn't ever offer her that, even if she decided she did want it. Not only was he incapable of it, but he also *couldn't* allow his relationship with Stella to ever become any more than the partnership he'd promised her because there were parts of him she didn't know. Deep, flawed parts of him he would never admit to anyone—pieces of him that would destroy Stella if she knew.

He pushed aside the guilt that knotted in his chest. He had forgiven himself that particular sin because he and his country needed Stella. It was necessary. Which meant he had to earn that trust his fiancée was demanding, prove to her they could make this work, while never making promises he couldn't keep.

Considering the fact that in three weeks the eyes of the world would be upon this country as he and Stella cemented ties between Akathinia and Carnelia, he had his work cut out for him.

CHAPTER SIX

KOSTAS STOOD LEANING against the blacked-out windows of the Bentley, jacket discarded, a dusk-driven breeze stealing across his skin. His oxygen-deprived brain had craved fresh air as he waited for Stella to appear for their dinner engagement, too many weeks of conference rooms and endless bickering about election minutiae clouding his brain. That and the seemingly endless pushback he was receiving on the hotel developments he was negotiating for the east coast of Carnelia.

It was enough to make a man question his sanity for attempting to take on this almost impossible job.

Tonight, however, would be enjoyable. With his wedding just a week away, he and Stella were joining Tassos Andropoulos, his best friend and best man, for dinner at a tiny, low-key restaurant in the city to discuss last-minute details. It was an establishment he knew well, whose proprietor would keep their presence hush-hush, a necessity considering the anticipation for his nuptials had reached a fever pitch. The madness descending over Carnelia was something he would be happy to see the back of.

The foreign media, scheduled to arrive this week to cover the lead-up to the wedding, were salivating over the celebrity-packed guest list, as were the people of Carnelia, who hadn't seen such an influx of famous visitors since the wedding of his grandmother Queen Cliantha. Their enthusiasm was heightened by the weeklong festivities scheduled around the ceremony, which included two days of national holidays to celebrate. He thanked the high heavens the only thing he had to do was show up.

Pulling in another deep breath of the clean, quiet air, he focused his attention on the entrance to the castle and his fiancée's imminent appearance, rather than the insanity to come. Punctuality was not one of Stella's virtues, but since she had so many others, he was willing to overlook it.

She had been picture-perfect in an appearance at the annual fig festival, winning over the farmers with her wit and charm as they served as the judges of the cake-baking competition featuring the star fruit, then doing the same at an official state dinner for the Italian prime minister as Carnelia officially reopened relations with that country.

Unfortunately, for his goal of creating a manageable stasis for his own relationship, the cool, composed Stella who had presented herself on those public occasions had been the same one to greet him every morning in the two weeks since their confrontation in the conservatory. He seemed to be an object of suspicion, to be avoided, while she wrapped her head around their relationship. He hoped the tiny but noticeable thawing in her manner toward him meant they were headed in the right direction.

His introspection came to a halt as Stella exited the front doors and came down the stairs in a cloud of exotic, sophisticated perfume. He was a fan of the scent as well as the dress she wore—a formfitting, knee-length cocktail number embroidered with some type of flower he couldn't identify.

"Sorry," she murmured, coming to a halt in front of

him, the careful smile that seemed to be her de facto response to him of late pasted on her lips.

"No, you aren't," he said easily, shifting away from the car, "or you'd be on time."

Oh. Those blue eyes sharpened. *It's going to be that kind of night?*

It's been that kind of fortnight.

Her lashes lowered in that reining in of emotion he was coming to hate.

"We should go," he murmured, sliding his fingers around the handle of the car door and opening it. She walked past him, sinking her bottom into the seat, then swinging those incredible legs of hers inside. His palm grazed the curve of her hip as he bent to tuck her in, the brief touch of his fingertips to her firm, delectable bottom eliciting the full stare of its owner.

He shut the door on her pensive face because there were some things a man simply couldn't resist and that had been one of them. Nodding at the driver, who was perched by the front of the car along with Darius and his own bodyguard, he walked around to the other side and slid in.

She eyed him from a safe distance away. "You are exhausted. You need sleep."

He rested his head against the back of the seat and closed his eyes. "Clone me. That would help."

"At least you'll be able to relax this evening with Tassos. I like him."

"All woman like Tassos. He's good-looking and he flies fast, dangerous planes."

"His occupation certainly doesn't hurt." Amusement laced her voice. "How did you two meet?"

"In military training. First here, then in England and

California. We were on the same path and we clicked. Then we were deployed together in the navy."

"He's the light to your dark," she said. "You are good foils for one another."

"Perhaps."

A silence. "You're upset about the editorial."

"*Frustrated* is a better description." The scathing piece by the business editor of the Carnelian daily newspaper this morning had felt like a betrayal. He'd unleashed the stranglehold his father had kept on the media as one of his first actions as king.

The editor had paid him back by describing him as an "unyielding force determined to push through modernization plans the people weren't ready for." "The new king," the piece had gone on to say, "is showing shades of his father."

"Why don't you meet with him?" Stella suggested. "It would be good to establish that relationship. Another key influencer."

He opened his eyes. "What's the point? He clearly doesn't comprehend or care about the facts."

"*Kostas.*" She shook her head. "There's been significant pushback on your plans from more than one group. You need to educate, but more than that, you need to *listen*. The more you push forward without doing that, the angrier they are going to become. If you don't want to lose the goodwill you've built up, you need to create some bridges."

He trained his gaze on her. "He accused me of having my father's *dictatorial tendencies*."

"Then prove him wrong." She shook her head. "He is not entirely incorrect in that portrayal. You *are* dogmatic. You see the world in black-and-white. You need to acknowledge the gray, find a middle ground."

Antagonism stiffened his shoulders. "It's the people who need to wake up. They all want the gain and no pain. *I* am trying to give them a future. If they are too short-sighted to recognize it, that's not my problem, it's theirs."

"It will be yours if they turn their backs on you."

Blood throbbed against his temples. Pushing his head back against the seat, he stared straight ahead. "I'm getting enough on all sides, Stella. I don't need it from you."

"Then why marry me? You said you wanted a partner, so here I am, telling you what you need to hear rather than what you want to hear."

His lashes fluttered closed. He had asked for that, yes. He just didn't need it right *now*. Nor did he need his fiancée agreeing with that damn editor. He couldn't believe she'd *gone* there, knowing who he was. What he was.

Stella considered her combustible fiancé as the car pulled up in front of the restaurant. Darius and Kostas's bodyguard got out first to scan the area. So much for her stress-free, enjoyable evening getting to know Tassos better. He was the one person, it seemed, who knew the king beyond a superficial level.

Kostas was like an explosive device, primed and ready to go off. Clearly the insane amount of pressure he was under was taking a toll, and how could it not? Still, she knew her role was to help guide him and she wasn't about to pull any punches for both their sakes. Not with General Houlis continuing to amass support behind the scenes, the frustrated public a perfect target for his efforts.

She let him cool off as their security declared the area secure and they were welcomed into the cozy little restaurant off a main avenue by the proprietor, who led them to an out-of-the-way table at the back, where the handsome, dark-haired, green-eyed Tassos sat waiting for them. He was, of course, busily engaged with their beautiful blonde waitress.

"Attempting to find a suitable bottle of wine," he informed them as he stood and gave Kostas a clap on the shoulder and Stella a kiss on both cheeks. "Any preferences?"

"Anything with alcohol in it," Kostas suggested, holding out Stella's chair and tucking her into the table.

Tassos gave him a mocking look. "I thought you gave that up with the monks?"

A half smile broke through her fiancé's stiffness. "There were certain habits I wasn't willing to give up."

Tassos asked the waitress to bring them a bottle of Chianti. "It's the sex I couldn't do without," he said, offering the departing blonde a smile full of promise. "That's where I derive my *tranquillity* from."

"Clearly you must be very tranquil, then," Kostas returned mockingly. "Have you decided who the lucky recipient will be for the wedding? We're seven days out."

"It's an issue," said Tassos, face deadpan. "There is an implicit assumption among women if you bring them to a wedding that it's serious. On the other hand," he said, a contemplative look on his face, "when the champagne is flowing, it's sure to be enjoyable. Maybe I should just take the waitress."

Stella shook her head at his arrogance. Tassos was good-looking and charming enough to get away with it. The blonde would likely trip over herself in her haste to say yes. It turned her thoughts to her current problem—her very arrogant fiancé's request for calmer waters in their relationship.

She had to let go of her antagonism toward him, she knew. Of the history that prevented them from moving forward and truly realizing this partnership because she knew in her heart they could be different if they had a fresh start, that they did have a strong mutual respect for each other. Perhaps it had been the reality of what she'd committed herself to that had been driving her aggression, the radical changes in her life, the loneliness she had felt without her siblings at her side, the tenuous situation she and Kostas were in. Not to mention her own conflicting feelings toward him.

But with her introspection had come clarity. She wanted this partnership to work; knew that together she and Kostas were more powerful than the sum of their parts. It was painful, hard work they were doing, but it was so worth it—she knew she could make a difference in this country's future. Felt she *had* a purpose. With her and Kostas's biggest challenges yet unscaled, he was right—a resolution was necessary. Some sort of relationship was necessary between them.

It had also been impossible not to admire the strong, powerful force of good her fiancé had been for his wounded country. He was still the larger-than-life figure she'd always thought he was, but she'd now accepted that he also made mistakes, as everyone did. Could they manage a real relationship together where she let down her guard and let him in while keeping love firmly out of the picture? She thought maybe they could.

She'd always considered Kostas incapable of opening up emotionally, but he had changed since his time in Tibet. He had talked to her about his past—yes, because he'd wanted her acquiescence, but still he had done it. Maybe he was capable of investing in a relationship— maybe he was capable of more. Maybe she had to take a risk and trust him as he'd suggested.

Tucking that away for future thought, she returned her attention to the conversation at hand. Her fiancé gradually lost his combustive edge in the presence of the ever-entertaining Tassos, who clearly knew how to handle him. She took mental notes. By the time their dinner plates were removed and a bottle of wine had been consumed, with liqueurs on the way, Kostas was almost human again. Then his phone rang.

"I have to take it," he apologized. "It may be a few minutes."

"Go." Tassos waved a hand at him. "Your sexy, intelligent fiancée is in safe hands."

Kostas slanted him a look that said that was debatable, then disappeared onto the terrace. Tassos sat back in his chair, cradling his wineglass in his hands. "He's agitated tonight."

"It's the editorial. I keep telling him communication is a two-way street, but you know what he's like. He thinks he knows best. Which he does… It's how he's executing that needs finessing."

"He struggles with his father's legacy." Tassos's gaze was frank. "More than anyone knows. He feels the pressure because of the duty that's so deeply ingrained in him—the responsibility for his father's misdirection. He ends up caring too much and internalizing the stress."

She nodded. "I know. I'm just not sure how to help him."

"I think you are. You aren't afraid of him, afraid to give him a different perspective. That's what he needs, that and someone who will stand by him and give him the unconditional love and support he's never had. Who lets him know he isn't alone."

"You have," she pointed out.

"Yes. But I'm not engaged to be married to him. That kind of bond is different." Resting his glass against his chin, he gave her a contemplative look. "He needs to see the light again. He needs to remember the world is a good place beyond everything he's been through."

A knot formed in her stomach, pulling her insides tight. Shame was its origin. The shame of being so horribly oblivious to the truth an apparently far-deeper-than-she'd-thought Tassos had just voiced.

"Yes," she said in a low voice, edged with emotion. "I agree."

He eyed her. "It must be complicated for you two. With what happened with Athamos…"

That might be the understatement of the year.

"*They* were complicated," he continued with a frown. "At each other's throats one minute, tight the next. Always the competition. But to have what happened happen? Kostas went off the rails. I've never seen him like that."

The knot in her stomach tightened. "What do you mean 'off the rails'?"

"I mean I didn't know if he was coming back from Tibet, mentally or physically. He wasn't communicating with anyone, not me, nor his father. He literally disappeared. When everyone was asking where Kostas was, why he wasn't intervening with Akathinia, not even the king knew where he was. When Idas fell ill, he had no idea if his son was going to assume the crown or not. The wolves were circling."

Thee mou. She bit her lip, a feeling of disbelief spreading through her. Had Kostas seriously been thinking of not coming back? Of *not* becoming king? It was so far from the man she knew and the duty he had lived by that it blew a hole in her brain.

"I can't even conceive of that."

Tassos swallowed his last sip of wine, then put down

the glass. "He hasn't flown since Athamos's death. Hasn't gone near a plane. Flying is his peace, his serenity."

She stared at him. "You think he isn't flying because of Athamos?"

"I think maybe he thinks he doesn't deserve to be happy."

"It was an *accident.*"

His gaze probed hers. "Is that how *you* saw it in the beginning?"

No. Her heartbeat thickened in her chest. But then again she had been so wrong about so many things when it came to Kostas, too caught up in her own anguish to consider what he might be going through, that she'd made a million assumptions.

A weight descended over her, a thick blanket of culpability she wasn't sure how to handle. "Like you said," she murmured, "it's complicated."

The pretty waitress arrived to deliver their liqueurs. Tassos waited until she disappeared before he spoke again. "Did Athamos ever tell you what happened between him and Kostas in flight school? The day they flew their first solo cross-country flight?"

She shook her head.

"It's an exercise all of us had to do as part of our flight school training. You fly the route first with an instructor, who takes you through the checkpoints and familiarizes you with the route. Then you fly it the next day by yourself. Kostas and Athamos were up there together, vying for best-pilot status. They were neck and neck at the time.

"Kostas was about half an hour ahead. Unfortunately for them, the weather deteriorated as the day went on. It was difficult to see the checkpoints and Athamos got lost. So lost he was dangerously low on fuel. He panicked and radioed for help. Kostas heard his calls, flew back, found him, took his wing and guided him back to the base."

She felt the blood drain from her face. "If he had run out of fuel…"

"They were both critically low on fuel by the time they touched down, Kostas worse than Athamos because he'd flown farther. He was flying on fumes by the end."

She set her glass down, hands shaking. "What happened afterward?"

"They were given a chance to refly the route. Athamos didn't want to. He was shaken up, crushed by his failure, frightened by what happened. He wanted to quit. Kostas talked him out of it."

She pressed her hand to her mouth, fighting to hold back the emotion welling up inside of her. "What did he say to him?"

"That every pilot makes mistakes and those mistakes define their career. That he had to dig down deep and go back up there—that he would be by his side the whole way but to quit was not an option."

"And he did."

"Yes."

Liquid fire burned the backs of her eyes. She blinked furiously, but this time she didn't manage to hold back as she had so many other times. Tears slid down her cheeks like silent bandits.

Tassos closed a hand over hers. "I didn't mean to make you sad. I'm telling you this so you understand…so you can understand Kostas better. It kills me every time I hear that damn story about the race because it's only one piece of what he and Athamos were. Only those two men know the truth of what happened that night and it's far more complicated than anyone knows."

And she had been the biggest judge of all. Anger at herself dueled with the need to make this right.

"Thank you," she murmured, "for telling me this. I needed to hear it."

If it wasn't a sign she needed to let go, then nothing ever would be. She needed to let go of *all of it*.

CHAPTER SEVEN

HAVING BEEN EFFECTIVELY blown off by her fiancé, who'd
gone off to work as soon as they'd returned to the castle
with that dark cloud around him again after the phone
call he'd received, Stella elected to go to bed. She was
too emotionally wrung-out from her evening to contem-
plate anything else.

She took a long soak in a bath in the rather garish,
outdated purple-and-gold marble bathroom that adjoined
her suite—any renovations would have to wait until the
key rooms were finished. Stella slipped into a nightgown,
picked up a book and took it to bed. But the more she
thought about her conversation with Tassos, the more
she didn't understand. Confusion mixed with frustration
in a caustic brew. Why hadn't Kostas told her about his
and Athamos's history? Why had he never attempted to
defend himself? How was she supposed to have a real
relationship with a man *she didn't even know*?

Throwing back the covers, she strode to the door,
flung it open and headed for Kostas's study. The light
that streamed across the stone floor from underneath the
door told her he was still working.

Fingers curling around the handle, she let herself inside. Kostas looked up from behind his desk, the hard
lines of his face haggard, his beautiful catlike eyes a

vivid beacon in the dim light. Dropping his gaze down over her, he made her suddenly aware of how see-through the ivory nightie she had on must be in the pool of light she stood in.

"This isn't a social visit," she snapped, rounding the desk to put herself in shadow. "I've come to talk."

"Pity," he murmured, his gaze eating her up. "I thought you might finally have come around."

She crossed her arms over her chest. "That would entail both of us entering this so-called relationship on equal footing, and since that isn't the case, we have work to do."

He threw down his pen and leaned back in the chair. "I'm assuming you're going to tell me why that isn't the case."

"Tassos told me about your cross-country test in flight school. About what you did for Athamos."

His mouth tightened. "So."

"So you saved his career, might have saved his life if he hadn't found his way out of that mess before he ran out of fuel, and you chose *not* to tell me?"

"He would have."

"No, Kostas, that isn't a given." She clenched her hands at her sides. "Why did you allow me to paint you the bad guy, to *damn you*, when there was so much more to the two of you?"

"Because it didn't make any difference. I needed to own my mistake."

"It *does* make a difference. It goes to who you are. The kind of man you are. The man I've always known you are."

A glimmer entered those dark, inscrutable eyes. "Don't go painting me a hero, Stella. I've already crushed your illusions once. I did what any pilot would have done in my position. As for not providing explanations, you didn't want to hear them."

"Because you waited a year and a half to tell me. Because my grief has been ruling me." She blew out a breath. "I owe you an apology."

"Just like that?"

"No, not *just like that*." She dropped her hands onto her hips. "Are you punishing yourself? Is that it? By pressing forward and not giving a damn what anyone thinks?"

His expression hardened. "Now who's psychoanalyzing?"

"Yes. It's my turn now. And you know what I've determined so far? You were always closed, Kostas, your focus was always on the endgame. The women you collected, your top gun status, your summa cum laude superiority—nothing was allowed to interfere with your vision, with *winning*. But with everything that's happened, you've locked yourself up and thrown away the key. You've decided you will save this country, come hell or high water, and that is your *penance*. You've given up your idealism for the very cynicism you accuse me of, when that is exactly what this country needs most."

His dark lashes lowered to half-mast. "What do you propose I do? Let the country wither away and die while we all hold on to our outdated, fatal visions of what we want to be?"

"No. You compromise. You dream *together*. I *see* you wanting to connect with the people, desperate to make them understand your vision, but in order to do that you have to show them you are one of them, just like your grandmother said. Right now, they aren't sure about that."

His gaze fell away from hers, a silence filling the room. He dropped his head into his hands, fingertips massaging his temples. She could feel the storm emanating from him, the loneliness, the frustration, the drive to make everything right. The need to never again be that five-year-old boy standing beside his father inspecting a military guard, bewildered and lost. It tore the heart right out of her.

Taking the last steps between them, she bent and framed his face in her hands, making him look at her. "I am willing to be all-in with this partnership with you, Kostas. I think we can be that unstoppable team you spoke of, that we can *do* this together. But if we're going to make this a real relationship, you need to give of yourself as much as you're asking of me. You have to show you're *capable* of being in a relationship for me to invest in you. For me to trust you. I need to know we are in this together."

His gaze darkened. "I've shared things with you. Things about my past."

"Yes," she agreed, "and I need you to keep doing that, to prove to me this is the right decision I'm making, because you were right about me—my past means I don't trust easily, I never have. But I do believe you are right, I do believe we can be different. I believe the respect we have for each other means something."

He rubbed a hand over the stubble on his jaw. "Being emotionally available isn't my forte, Stella. It never has been. But I will do my best. I am committed to making this work."

She straightened, hands falling away from his face. "Trust, transparency and complete honesty between us are the rules."

A play of emotion flickered in those dark eyes. She wondered which of the three things she'd listed had caused it, because they needed all of them if this was going to work.

"All right," he said. "Agreed."

She blew out a breath. "Okay, then."

His gaze slid over her. Settled on the thrust of her breasts under the thin material of the silk negligee. Electricity sparkled across her skin like white lightning, heat pooling low in her abdomen at his blatant perusal. She bit her lip as her nipples betrayed her and hardened to tight peaks.

"You want to come here and seal the deal with a kiss?"

A part of her knew it would be a big mistake. Another part knew it was inevitable. An intimate relationship between them was a given with the need to produce an heir. She couldn't deny she didn't want him, hadn't always wanted him. Perhaps a test run would be a good idea to see how hard it was going to be to keep a handle on her feelings for him. And it was just one kiss...

Kostas hooked an arm around her waist and tugged her down onto his lap. She sucked in a breath, pressing a hand to his ripped, rock-hard chest. His big, hard body underneath her was a hot brand she couldn't ignore, leashed, pure masculine power that told her she was playing with fire, that perhaps this hadn't been a very good idea at all.

He curved a palm around her neck and brought her head down to his. His mouth took hers in an exquisitely soft, gentle kiss, butterfly-light, easy to extract herself from. Except she didn't because it destroyed some of the connections in her brain.

She allowed herself to sink into it, to discover whether the kiss on the dance floor had really been that magical, exactly *how* dangerous he was to her. Angling his mouth over hers, he deepened the pressure, turned it into a soul-destroying exploration that sent more of those little quakes through her.

So it had been magical. She should have ended it there,

should have called the experiment done, but then he slid his tongue along the crease of her mouth and demanded entry. Too caught up in the sensual web he was weaving to object, she opened for him and the kiss turned breathtakingly intimate; a relearning of each other on a deeper level.

Not hungry, but staking a claim instead. *Sealing the deal.* Her stomach muscles coiled as the smooth, hot length of his tongue slid against hers. Stroked her languidly, provocatively, like a bit cat on the prowl. The hand he held at the small of her back drew her closer until she was plastered against him, breasts crushed against his chest.

He trailed his lips along her cheek, along the line of her jaw, working his way toward the sensitive spot just below her ear. She gasped as he brought his tongue into play in an erotic caress that made her shiver. Fingers clutching the fabric of his shirt, she arched her neck back as he licked his way higher to take possession of her lobe, sucking it into the heat of his mouth.

Thee mou, but he knew what he was doing. A low moan escaped her as he closed his teeth around the tender skin, scored her vulnerable flesh, her insides contracting with her reaction to him. He could take her now and she'd be ready for him.

She was fairly sure he knew it as he lifted his mouth from her and brushed a thumb across her cheek. "One kiss as promised, *glykeia mou*. The next move is up to you."

She blinked. "What do you mean?"

"It means I'm not touching you again until you ask me to."

A bizarre sense of disappointment sliced through her. "What about the heir you so urgently require?"

"It can wait."

"And if I never come to you?"

He set her on her feet. "That doesn't even rank on the scale of probability."

Kostas watched his fiancée walk out of the room, an emotional tsunami that had hit, then departed. She had been ready to crawl into his bones. He had been ready for it, too. His erection pounded with every beat of his heart, craving satisfaction, but since his fiancée had finally agreed to commit to this partnership in every way, he would gladly suffer through it.

With their wedding happening in a week, madness about to descend around them, they needed this consensus. Having Stella share his bed, and he had no doubt she would after the response she'd just given him, would allow both of them to get this chemistry out of their system. Produce the heir his country so desperately needed. Allow him to return a singular focus to the job at hand— right-siding Carnelia.

It would have been better, however, for that story of him and Athamos to have never come out. Stella insisted on seeing him as a hero—as the ideal she had always wanted, *needed* him to be, when in fact, he was far from it. He'd gone so far as to deliberately hurt her all those years ago to dissuade her of that vision and still she had persisted with it.

Guilt clawed through him, sinking into his insides. He pushed it aside with ruthless precision. He had been careful what he'd promised her. Trust, transparency and complete honesty—*those things* he could offer. With his one necessary sin of omission.

Restlessness drove him to his feet. Crossing to the bar, he poured himself the nightcap he'd missed at the restaurant. Turning, he leaned against the sideboard and took a long gulp. Today's high-profile, public lashing had flattened him…stung him with its betrayal. Made him wonder about his country's will to pull itself from the ashes.

He had spent his life nurturing a dream of democracy for Carnelia. Was five weeks away from attaining it. Yet, history was full of examples of the offspring of dictators who had set out to be different, with bright visions for their country, only to be defeated by the forces stacked against them. As if they'd never stood a chance. He was not going to be one of them.

Backtracking on his plans would poke holes in his leadership, holes General Houlis could exploit. The general was a man who wanted to hang him before the elections ever happened.

He lifted the glass to his mouth and took another sip of the whiskey. His father's voice filled his head, as clear as if he'd been standing in this room, one he'd once presided over, delivering one of his sermons.

A great vision is one that must be believed in without reservation, preserved at all costs. Any show of weakness means it all falls apart.

His mouth twisted. His father might have been driven by misguided and, at times, warped ideas, but he had been right about that particular one. Any show of weakness by him would allow his enemies to pounce. He was never going to let that happen.

CHAPTER EIGHT

THE ANCIENT CHURCH bells rang in Carnelia as they would on the quarter hour until the royal wedding took place in the Marcariokastro chapel in just under sixty minutes. With each deep, resonant gong of the bells, Stella's stomach pulled tighter, a rock-hard fist she couldn't unclench.

Not because of the five hundred guests preparing to attend her wedding. Not because of the vow she was about to make to king and country. Not even because General Houlis and his dangerous group of disciples would be in the audience. Instead, her nerves stemmed from the fact that in just over an hour she would not only pledge to stand by Kostas's side forever, but she would also share his bed.

"Right." Satisfied with the job she'd done, the makeup artist fussing over her face declared her a masterpiece. "I'm leaving tiny backups," she said, gesturing to the dresser. "Smudge-proof lipstick and powder. Your mascara is waterproof so crying shouldn't be a problem."

She smiled her thanks. She was fairly certain that wouldn't be an issue. She felt frozen, as if she'd been carved out of marble. Wondering if she'd made a huge mistake agreeing to embark on a real marriage with Kostas, to have an intimate relationship with a man she was still sure had the ability to tear her heart out.

She had, however, made a promise to Kostas and she intended on following through on it. Intended on putting everything she had into making this partnership— their relationship—a success. Part of that commitment included providing Kostas with an heir, and since that electric kiss in his study had proved chemistry wasn't going to be a problem, she had decided to simply get it out of the way.

It made sense, after all, to consummate their relationship on their wedding night. Symbolically it was a fresh start for them. All she had to do was ensure her complex, reemerging feelings for her fiancé never went past the mutual respect and partnership they had promised each other.

A rock lodged itself in her throat. Simpler said than done. She wondered what it was going to be like to set this thing loose between her and Kostas. The thought was equally soul-shifting and terrifying.

Sofía bustled through the door with her dress, having made a tiny, last-minute alteration, with Alex close on her heels. "All done," her sister-in-law announced breathlessly.

Discarding her robe, Stella stood and lifted her arms to allow Sofía to settle the dress down over her in a rustle of satin. An unexpected wave of emotion swept over her. It was gorgeous. Her dream dress on the odd day she'd ever imagined herself getting married.

"Oh, Sofía," Alex breathed. "It's perfect. You are a genius."

It *was* genius. The romantic, off-the-shoulder, fit-and-flare satin gown made the most of her slim figure, the lace overlay softening an otherwise sleek, unadorned silhouette. "You don't need any more with your strong look," Sofía had said earlier. Which had meant, in reality, the square line of her jaw and her prominent nose, but she'd been okay with that assessment. She was aware she wasn't beautiful in the traditional sense and was more frequently labeled *striking* by the tabloids.

She gave Sofía a hug. "It's amazing. *Efharisto.*"

"*You* are amazing." Her sister-in-law squeezed her tight. "Carnelia is lucky to have you."

"As is Akathinia to have you." She kissed Sofía on the cheek.

And then, all too soon, the moments had flown by. With her delicate sparkly gold heels on, jewelry in place, including a heavy sapphire-and-diamond necklace Kostas had given her last night that had been Queen Cliantha's, Stella had an awkward last moment with her mother that didn't end up being so bad because Queen Amara looked so truly happy for her.

It was *time*.

Kostas waited for his bride under the fresco-emblazoned dome of the eighteenth-century Marcariokastro royal chapel, Tassos at his side. Beyond the stunning centerpiece of the Venetian-inspired chapel, the guests sat in the main gallery, presided over by a massive gold filigree chandelier that bathed the room in a muted glow.

Every manner of politician, royalty, aristocrat and celebrity was in attendance. They had come, according to the international press, to see the dawn of a new age in Carnelia, the coming of Camelot. He wasn't sure how long that label was going to stick after that damning editorial and the increasing public discontent that had risen in the wake of it over his modernization plans, but he was determined to stay the course. The future of his country depended on it.

A flash of white appeared at the entrance to the chapel

as the strains of Vivaldi's *Four Seasons* began. Jessie's three-year-old daughter, in a beautiful white dress with a red bow, started down the aisle and was followed by her mother in an elegant bloodred gown Sofía had designed. Next came the designer herself, vivacious and stunning in a red gown of a different style, followed by Aleksandra.

"All married..." Tassos sighed. "You could have allowed me just one."

"You don't need the help," Kostas countered, appreciating the comic relief. "You acquired your blonde waitress."

"She's a short-term rental." Tassos, sharp in a black tux and red bow tie, flicked him a glance. "If I had one like the one you're marrying today, I would happily trade her in as a permanent addition."

A message. *Appreciate what you have.* It was unnecessary. He had no doubts he was making the right choice today. In his duty and the woman he'd chosen. Stella was his match in every way. Fearless, passionate and strong enough to accomplish the most impossible dream with him.

Duty, however, didn't explain how his heart rose to his throat as a ripple went through the crowd. Stella had appeared at the entrance to the chapel on Nikandros's arm, the train of her dress flowing behind her. Her hair was caught up in a sophisticated twist that illuminated the arresting lines of face, her dress an elegant, perfect foil for her beautiful body, the necklace he'd given her glittering around her neck.

All he could do was stare. The desire to possess her, to mark her as his, moved through him as an inescapable force. To claim what he hadn't taken ten years ago but had desired above all else.

He wasn't sure what he'd expected in return, which

Stella might show up today as she walked down the aisle: the fiery, combative version who had greeted him in Barbados, or the cool, aloof creature who had driven him crazy for weeks, or the warm Stella he'd witnessed of late, intent on making them work. But as she and Nikandros walked down the aisle, Stella's features distant, untouchable, the smile on her face perfect, but more a mask than a real form of expression, he knew exactly what he'd gotten.

She could have been attending a coronation, any official occasion other than her own wedding, she was just that removed. A wave of infuriated heat spread through him, despite his own doubts about his ability to give her what she needed. *They were not going backward, not now.*

The music at a crescendo, the pair reached him. Stella's beautiful eyes, as electric a Constantinides blue as her brother's, were cool blue sapphires as they came to rest on him, about a dozen layers of that ice he despised painted over her. Transferring his attention to Nikandros, he shook his hand as the king gave his sister away. Enfolding Stella's slim fingers in his, the slight tremor he found there threw him yet again.

"Nervous about devoting your life to me?" he murmured in her ear.

"Hardly."

"Then why is your hand trembling?"

"It's a big day."

He pondered that comment as they turned to the priest, the guests sat and the service began. The joining of the hands, which they'd already accomplished, was followed by the service of betrothal, in which they exchanged their rings, and the procession of the crowns.

He spoke his vows to Stella in a clear, unwavering

tone that spoke of his confidence in them. Her icy, cool demeanor slipped slightly, her eyes turning a deep violet blue as she spoke her vows to him, her elocution perfect in the cavernous chapel.

The priest completed the benediction of their union, declaring them man and wife. Kostas curved an arm around his bride's waist and drew her to him. His touch, as he cupped her jaw in his fingers, was light, but firm, staking his claim in that way that was irresistible to him, his kiss as he captured her satiny soft lips a demonstration of how very good this was going to be between them—in every way.

Stella needed time to recover from that calamitous kiss Kostas had given her that had promised so much. She got it as they exited the chapel to applause and cheers amid a contemporary, hauntingly beautiful version of "Hallelujah."

After being saluted with handfuls of rice and good wishes, they headed to the gardens for the official photographs. They seemed to take forever in the bright sunshine, pushing the throb in her head to a full-on ache. Jessie produced some aspirin from her bridal emergency kit that Stella downed with a bottle of water, as opposed to the champagne that was already flowing among the others. By the time they'd returned to the ballroom for dinner and she had eaten a few bites of the roasted lamb and her favorite, the spinach-and-feta pies, she was feeling better. Now if only she could diminish her ever-present awareness of the man sitting beside her.

Speeches were held throughout the courses, by family and dignitaries alike. It wasn't until dessert was served that she and Kostas stood to deliver their toasts to each other. Kostas, devastating in military dress, went first, a glass of champagne in his hand. His eyes on her, he praised his choice of bride—for her duty to country, her valuable philanthropic work, her beauty, wit and intelligence.

Warmed by what she knew to be genuine appreciation on his part, she stood to do her toast, unsure if she could match Kostas's brilliant endeavor with anything better. But she had a story to tell.

"When I was six," she said, focusing on the crowd, "I met a boy named Kostas. It was a hot summer day and I was climbing a tree in the gardens of the Akathinian palace, mad at my parents for something I can't remember now. I, along with my brothers, were supposed to be entertaining the children of some visiting guests, but I was too angry and couldn't make myself do it.

"I was halfway up the tree when this voice, this little boy's voice, reached me. He asked me what I, a girl, was doing climbing a tree. I sat down on a branch, secured my perch and told him that I was going to do great things one day, so why not climb a tree? This look passed over his face, this thoughtful look. Then he climbed up the tree, sat down beside me and told me his name."

Tears, unexpected and disconcerting, stung her eyes. Swallowing, she blinked them back. "He told me he, too, was going to do great things someday. He was going to become king, like his father, except maybe he would be a little bit nicer to the people. I agreed with him that that would be a good thing and we sat there, sometimes talking, sometimes not, for a long time until our parents came to flush us out.

"And you know, as children, we sometimes have dreams that fade with time. We realize we want to be a doctor instead of a football player, a lawyer instead of a ballerina, but the little boy I met turned into a young man and then a man and those dreams never died. I was awed by his ability to focus—to never forget he wanted to make the world a better place. It has inspired me in so many ways with my own life."

She turned to her husband. "To watch Kostas carry out his dreams, to witness his passion for Carnelia, to *see* this country shine with a brilliant future because of it, only solidifies what I always knew because of him. If you allow yourself to hope, to *believe* this world can be a better place, anything is possible.

"And so tonight," she said, swallowing past the lump in her throat and lifting her glass to the man who affected her on such a profound level, "I give a toast to my husband and say thank you. I and Carnelia are very lucky to have you."

Kostas stood as applause swept the room, the crowd rising with him. His eyes were dark, full of emotion for a man who claimed to feel little and suspiciously bright as he held his glass up to hers. It made her wonder if she would give the waterproof mascara a run for its money.

He bent his head to hers. "Always trying to make me the hero, Stella?"

She shook her head. "Always trying to put words in my mouth, Kostas? I called you an inspiration because you are that to me."

He pressed his lips to her cheek. Dragged his mouth to her ear. "I can't believe you remember that story. You forgot, however, the part where I offered you half of my lollipop. It goes to the gentleman in me."

She smiled. "I didn't. But to be honest, Kostas, I never was much interested in the gentleman part."

A pause. "Is that a request, Mrs. Laskos?"

"Why don't you try it and find out?"

Her stomach dissolved into complete chaos after that.

They took to the dance floor for their first dance, her fingers enfolded in his, his hand at her waist. Then there was only heat between them, a slow, languorous, deadly conflagration that turned her bones to mush.

When the others joined them, the dance floor packed with bodies, Kostas's hand dropped lower on her hip, pulling her into the muscular length of him. It was just barely an appropriate hold, one that telegraphed exactly where this night was headed.

Her breath trapped in her chest, she joined the riotous dancing—the Orea Pou Enai H Nifi Mas, which the wedding party danced in a circle in honor of her, the Kalamatiano, which Stella led, and the Hasapiko, her favorite.

Her headache thankfully receded. She got herself a glass of champagne and then another in an attempt to quiet the anticipation fizzing in her blood. Tassos turned out to be a demon on the dance floor, of course. She danced the night away with him, Alex, Sofía, Jessie and Aristos, aware of her husband's dark stare when she did so with the latter. A feeling of satisfaction spread through her. A little jealousy never hurt, not when it came to a man like Kostas, who was used to having everything he desired.

The clock struck midnight. It was as if an invisible line had been crossed. Kostas murmured something to the wedding planner, retrieved her from the dance floor and led her to the exit. The room was still boisterous and loud, but all she could hear was the pounding of her heart.

CHAPTER NINE

Why wasn't there air in this room?

Stella kicked her shoes off in the newly renovated master suite that had been transformed into a sumptuous, warm retreat by their genius of a designer, retaining the room's exposed stone walls and medieval ambience.

Plush, comfortable chairs formed a sitting area overlooking the tall windows. A mahogany canopy bed with intricately crafted pillars draped in gold brocade overlooked it, with a separate area at the far end of the room for dressing.

It was dreamy, gorgeous, but right now it seemed *claustrophobic*.

She walked to the French doors and threw them open. The cool, crisp air floating down off the mountains kissed her overheated skin. Drawing in a deep breath, she stood, looking out at the rugged, forbidding landscape, so harsh compared to Akathinia's sparkling, gilded beauty. It only underscored the different world she now lived in; how that world was shifting beneath her feet.

Her pulse ticked at an elevated rate she couldn't seem to regulate, a heat consumed her cheeks and her knees felt weak. Crazy, because she'd had sex before, she knew how this worked. But she was also aware it was going to be different, very different with Kostas. He touched an elemental part of her no one else ever had.

A skitter across her skin was the only notice she had before strong arms slid around her waist and pulled her back against a warm male body, one big enough to secure her compliance with anything he chose to do to her. But she knew Kostas would never have to resort to that with a woman. His strength would be used only for pleasure. *Hers*.

His lips found the sensitive skin below her ear. Her swift intake of breath was all too revealing.

"Why are you so nervous?"

Because the last time she'd put herself in this position he'd cruelly rejected her. *A decade ago, Stella. Time to get over it.* And yet still it hurt.

She gave him a half truth. "Sex is an intimate thing. It's hard for me to remain unaffected by it."

"Despite your determination to do so." He set his mouth to her shoulder, teeth scraping over her sensitive skin. "Is that what today was all about? Remaining unaffected by me?"

A shudder raked through her. "What do you mean?"

He sank his teeth into her skin, a tiny nip meant to punish. "I mean the return of the aloof, distant Stella I dislike. She disappears tonight, *yineka mou*. Those layers of ice you like to hide behind? *Gone*."

She struggled to regulate her pounding heart as his tongue laved the tiny bite he'd administered. "So I can take care of those *needs* you talked about?"

"No," he said throatily, "so I can take care of *yours*. You want this so badly you can taste it, *moro mou*, but you aren't sure how to engage."

So utterly true. Her stomach hollowed out, a shiver rippling across her skin. She took a deep breath, attempting to regain control. "I bought some lingerie…I should go put it on."

"We don't need lingerie, Stella." His mouth scored her other shoulder, sending another wave of shivers dancing across her skin. "The chemistry we share is more than enough."

Apparently so. "I bought it especially for you," she protested, her voice raspy. "You don't want to see it?"

"What color is it?"

"*Not* red."

"Pity." He reached up and unzipped her dress, pulling the metal slide down past the small of her back to her hips, where a tiny hook held the dress together. Undoing that, too, he ran a possessive hand up her spine, his caress a clear declaration of ownership. "Go. Put your armor on if you need to."

Finding refuge from her exploding pulse in the luxurious dressing area she and the designer had fashioned with deep walk-in closets, she lifted the dress over her head, hung it up like the precious piece that it was, then exchanged her nondescript, line-minimizing underwear for a beautiful sapphire silk baby doll and its matching panties.

The nightie came just to the top of her thighs, the lace cutouts at the sides hinting at the curves of her breasts and hips. It might be the armor Kostas had so astutely described it as, but it made her feel sexy and desirable, gave her the confidence she needed right now.

Pulling the dozens of pins out of her hair and running her fingers through it, she removed her jewelry and gave her still perfect makeup a once-over. She was ready. Of course, *ready* was a relative term. How could she ever really be *ready*?

Anticipation sizzling in her veins, she returned to the

bedroom. Kostas had taken off his tie, leaving him in a crisp white shirt he'd partially unbuttoned and dark trousers. His gaze shifted from the cuff links he was removing to her. Setting the gold pieces on the dresser, he turned and leaned back against the wood, the heat in his catlike eyes licking at her skin like a flame.

"Come here."

Her legs continued to evade full functionality—she felt vastly incompetent as she moved toward him. When she was within striking distance, he snaked an arm around her waist and pulled her into him with a swiftness that stole her breath.

Setting his big hands on the back of her bare thighs, he swept them up over the curve of her bottom to her waist. Fingers tightening, he lifted her onto the dresser, perching her on the edge while he cleared its contents with his free hand. Coins, cuff links and various other paraphernalia scattered to the floor, metal skimming across stone. Her heart hammered in her ears as she stared up at him. He was all dominant, aggressive male.

She had asked for this.

A slow burn worked its way across his olive-skinned cheeks. He was just as caught up in the moment as she was, she realized, just before he captured a chunk of her hair, tilted her head back and took her mouth in a kiss that was surprising in its gentle edge. Breathing into him, she rested her hands on his waist and returned it. Kiss for kiss, they exchanged intimacies until her entire body was pliant, melting, utterly his to command.

Opening to the heat of his tongue, her palm slid up to brace against his chest as he invaded, stroking deep inside her, forecasting how intimately he wanted to know her body. Dark and heady, the erotically charged essence of him made her toes curl.

Mouths separating, they sought air. Kostas rested his forehead against hers, his breathing rough. "Do you understand how badly I wanted you that night? How hard it was for me to put you on the other side of that door? I felt like I'd walked into the Garden of Eden and been told to keep my hands to myself."

"I didn't tell you that."

"I was wiser than you."

No, you weren't. It should have been with you. She kept that thought to herself as she leaned forward to kiss him again.

"No." He pushed her back until her hands braced themselves on the wood. *Utterly at his mercy.* "Stay put."

Her heart roared in her ears. His gaze settled on the rise and fall of her chest. The peaks of her breasts were hard, betraying points beneath the transparent silk. Bending, he took a hard peak into the heat of his mouth, sucking her deep inside. Alternating that excruciatingly delicious caress with gentle nips of his teeth, then soothing laves of his tongue, he sent liquid heat pooling between her thighs.

A low moan escaped her throat. He switched his attention to her other nipple, engorged and waiting for him now, administering the same exquisite torment until her low whimpers became an urgent plea.

Lifting his mouth from her breast, he clasped her hips and dragged her forward. His long fingers left a searing imprint on that sensitive, smooth, most intimate flesh. He took her mouth as he traced the inside edges of her panties with his thumbs. It was close, but not close enough to where she wanted him to touch her. A low mewl left her throat.

Abandoning the kiss, he took hold of the sides of her panties and stripped them off her, Stella lifting her hips to help him. His big hand cupped her hot, aching flesh in the most possessive of caresses. She gasped as a lightning bolt of sensation tore through her.

Sliding his other palm beneath her hips, his eyes held hers as he parted her slick, smooth flesh and filled her with one of his big, long fingers. She was wet, took him easily, her muscles clenching around him. It was good. *Too good.* She closed her eyes, a shudder raking through her.

He withdrew and filled her again, setting up a smooth rhythm that had her hips chasing his hand. The pressure inside her built fast and hard, her nails digging into the wood.

"I'm big," he murmured in her ear, his breath a heated caress. "You have to be ready for me. Would you like to come like this for me first?"

The last question was part purr, part tease, the animal in him in full evidence. Her cheeks flamed, her tongue struggling to find itself as the pleasure washed over her.

"I need an answer."

"Yes." Thee mou, yes. Her gaze found his. "Do you always talk like this?"

"Always. It's how I know I'm giving a woman pleasure."

Oh, my.

"There is another condition."

"What?"

"You have to watch. That part is for me."

She opened her eyes. He rewarded her with deeper, harder strokes. It was like getting lost in a storm, watching her pleasure written across his beautiful amber eyes, every moan, every whimper she let go reflected back at her. Her insides tightened as he worked her, pushing her toward orgasm, but every time she got close, he slowed it down and teased her with shallower strokes, keeping her release maddeningly out of reach.

"Is that good?" he asked, leaning forward to kiss her.

"So good."

"You want me to let you come?"

"Yes."

Drawing back, he withdrew his finger, then came inside of her with two. Thick and powerful, his fingers stretched her, filled her, tearing an animal-like moan from her throat. *So insanely good.*

"Please."

He was intent on pulling her apart. Intent on dismantling every single one of her defenses. She saw it in his eyes. He must have decided he'd accomplished his goal because he increased his rhythm then. She felt feverish, consumed by the sensations he was lavishing on her, her hips matching him stroke for stroke. When he slipped his thumb over the tight bundle of nerves at the core of her, his eyes darkening with purpose, and stroked her with a single, deliberate movement, she screamed.

The room blacked out around her.

Kostas carried a limp, sated Stella to the bed, setting her down beside it. Satisfaction pulsed through him at her explosive release. He had intended on breaking down every one of her walls, shattering that ice-cold composure she'd been wearing all day. Instead, her beautifully uninhibited response had taken him apart.

That she *affected* him was an understatement. Stella's impact on him had always been like a critical blood transfusion, injecting a life—a *need*—in him that escaped the boundaries of the rigidly held control he prized and made him want more. Made him want to *be* more; to be a flesh-and-blood man, capable of all the human emotion he'd never allowed himself.

She had been the only thing making him feel alive these past few weeks when taking on this rebellious, wounded country had seemed beyond any one man's ability, a constant, determined presence who had grounded him with the power of her tenacity. But thinking he could ever be the man Stella needed or wanted beyond the respect and affection he'd promised her was a recipe for disaster. Better to be realistic about what this relationship was—a partnership with intense, sexual chemistry.

Pushing his mind firmly back into realistic territory, he swept his gaze over her. All long limbs and slim curves, her golden skin gleaming in the light, hair mussed from his hands, she reminded him of an ancient Greek goddess: strong, brave, fearless. *Almost* fearless.

The flush darkening her cheeks drew his eye. Raising his hand, he trailed the back of his knuckles across the stain of color. "What?"

"Your body is a work of art. I want to see you."

Need clawed at his insides, swift and hard. "It's yours now, *glykeia mou*," he said huskily, capturing her hand and carrying it to the erection that swelled the front placket of his trousers. "For use immediately, *urgently*, in fact."

Heat blazed in her beautiful blue eyes. Spreading her palm wide, she traced the size and shape of him as he moved her fingers over his heat. A low, rough word escaped him as he arched into her touch. "Undress me."

She moved her fingers to the top button of his shirt, working her way down, the brush of her fingertips against his skin setting him on fire. Grasping hold of the collar of his shirt, she pushed it off his shoulders and let it drop to the floor. Feminine appreciation lit her gaze as it traveled over him. "You are insanely beautiful."

His mouth curved. "Should a man take that as a compliment?"

"Yes." The rasp in her voice made his heart thump against his chest.

Her fingers moved to his belt. She unbuckled it, then undid the button of his pants and slid down the zipper. His erection throbbed with every beat of his heart, hard and painfully ready to have her. He hadn't had a woman in over a year—since everything had fallen apart—but he knew it was the woman touching him that elicited his need, awakened his hunger, not the time that had passed.

She sank her fingers into the waistband of his trousers and worked them over his hips and to the floor. He stepped out of them, adding his close-fitting black boxers to the pile. Her eyes were riveted to the jutting erection that skimmed his abdomen, fascination warring with… *apprehension*?

Curving an arm around her waist, he caught her against him. "You saw me that night in my bed."

Long, golden-tipped lashes hid her gaze from him, but not before he saw a flash of something in all that blue fire. The remnant of the wound from that night? A part of him knew it was better if he left it alone. *Safer*. But he couldn't stand to watch her hurt.

Cupping her bottom, he brought her closer, until the length of his erection pressed against her belly, imprinting her with his need. "I've never wanted a woman more than I wanted you that night, *yineka mou*, not since and not now."

Her gaze darkened to a deep, indigo blue. "Never?"

He knew exactly who she was thinking about—the jealousy staining her eyes was crystal clear. Cassandra, however, as stunning as she was, had never touched him like this woman did.

"Never," he said, sliding his hands up the backs of her thighs and over her bottom, lifting the wispy, sexy piece of silk as he went, up and over her head. Tossing it to the floor, he rested his hands on her hips and drank her in. Her breasts were beautiful, high and taut, with rose-colored peaks, her hips delicately curved atop long, sexy legs he had pictured wrapped around him so many times he was aching with the thought of it. *She* was the work of art.

Lowering his mouth to hers, he brushed a single, hot caress across her lips, the palm he held at her bottom bringing her closer, getting her used to the press and slide of his body against hers. Skin-to-skin contact, the most intimate foreplay there was. When her lips clung to his, his name slipping softly from her lips, he picked her up and deposited her on the bed. Coming down over her, he ran a finger from breast to hip, her stomach muscles contracting beneath his touch. She was tense, edgy, despite the release he'd given her.

Closing his palm around her thigh, he spread her wide. Her eyes were liquid blue fire as she stared up at him. Dropping his gaze, he took her in. Beautifully open to him, she made his mouth go dry.

"Kostas." Her gaze willed his back up to hers.

"I like looking at you. *All* of you, Stella." He circled her wet, pliable flesh with his thumb, coming to rest on her core. Pressing down, he played her in sensual circles that made her hips arch up to meet his touch. "You're like a perfect, pink shell waiting to be discovered," he murmured, a raspy edge to his voice. "I'd use my mouth on you if I didn't need to be inside you so badly."

The sharp hiss of air she took in pleased him. Cupping

the back of her thigh, he wrapped one of her beautiful, elegant legs around his waist. Exposed to him, *ready* for him in a way that made his blood heat, he palmed himself and brought the flared head of his erection to her most intimate flesh. With more control than he thought he had left in him, he slid inside, giving her body time to adjust to the size and breadth of him. She exhaled, fingers clutching the velvet coverlet.

"Easy," he murmured. "We take it slow."

She took a deep breath, then another. Her body softened, melted around him. He eased forward another inch, then another. Arching her hips, she struggled to accommodate him, her tight channel clutching and rejecting him all at the same time. Hanging on by a thread, his pulsing body begging for release, he leaned forward and brushed his lips over hers. "You're so tight, *yineka mou*. So good. So sweet."

She nipped at his lip. Allowing her the distraction, he slid his hand between their bodies and rubbed his thumb over the swollen center of her. Caressed her as he whispered earthy, sexy words in her ear. Burying her fingers in his hair, she gave beneath him, her body relaxing. Finally, he was buried deep inside her.

Unsheathed by a condom for the first time with a woman, he absorbed the hot, wet velvet encasing him. She was like a tight, silken glove, the lush clenching of her muscles around him as her body expanded to take him the most erotic sensation he'd ever experienced.

Her eyes fluttered open. "Kostas," she gasped, "you're so big. I can feel you everywhere."

"I can feel *you* everywhere, *moro mou*." His gaze tangled with hers. "So strong, so passionate, you make me so hot for you, Stella."

She bit her lip. The overload of emotion he read in her

reverberated through him, touched him in a deep place he'd thought unreachable, because he felt it, too.

"Slowly," she whispered. "I want to feel every inch of you."

The huskily issued command was nearly the end of him, but somehow he managed to move in brutally restrained strokes; teasing, caressing movements that made her writhe against him. "You like that?" he rasped, rotating his hips. "You like that I fill you up?"

"So good," she moaned. "Don't stop."

He brought his mouth to hers, nipping at the plush curves as he pushed deeper, harder, inside her, giving her all he had. Her body rippled around him; tempted his self-control. Still he held back, his palm sliding beneath her buttock to lift her higher so he could find the spot that would give her the deepest, most intense orgasm.

"Right there," he breathed in her ear. "I can feel you tightening around me, Stella *mou*. Come for me."

A low moan ripped from her throat. "Kostas…"

He gripped her hips tighter, penetrating her body with deliberate, forceful thrusts that had her contracting around him. Digging her nails into his buttocks, she threw her head back, a sharp cry leaving her throat as her body clenched his in a long, hot pull that shattered him. Bracing his hands on either side of her, he let go, spilling himself inside of her.

The intimacy of it blew every emotion he'd ever had to smithereens—the giving of his life force to this woman, who in turn gave hers to him.

Long minutes later as his wife lay sleeping in his arms, the same state of being remained elusive for Kostas. Sleep had once come easily to him, a gift as his *yaya* had called it, an escape from the complexities of his life, but as the

years had passed and his father's manic phases had escalated, plunging the country into disarray, a solid night's
rest had eluded him. How could he rest when he was torn
in a dozen different directions? When his father was a
madman terrorizing his neighboring countries? When
his people were suffering?

When no decision had ever seemed like the right one.

He would have woken Stella and lost himself in her
addictive warmth again, but a part of him needed distance, the distance he had always craved when people got
too close. When his life seemed too complex to manage
any other way.

Sliding out of bed, he dressed and went down the hall
to his office, where he read the latest security report that
had come in on General Houlis's activity. The man who
had just wished he and Stella the best of luck for their
future happiness in an award-worthy performance was
growing increasingly desperate as the elections loomed
and his window of opportunity diminished.

If he was going to make a play for control of Carnelia,
he would need to do it soon. When that might be was unclear according to Kostas's eyes and ears on the ground.

Grimacing, he tossed the report aside. He was hoping
it would never come to pass; that Houlis would realize
the time for change had come to this country. But his security team was preparing contingency plans in case the
general did elect to go for the jugular.

He leaned back in his chair, rubbing a palm over the
coarse stubble on his chin. He should be focusing on the
threat to his country, to his own personal safety. Instead,
his head remained on the woman who lay sleeping in his
bed—his wife, whose armor had come off tonight, prov-
ing she was every bit the vulnerable, passionate woman
he'd known existed underneath all those protective layers.

Watching her walk down that aisle today, deliver that emotional toast, had touched a piece of him he hadn't even known existed. Taking her to bed, unleashing the passion that blazed between them, had only intensified those feelings; deep, uncharted ones he knew he should smother, the very ones he could never have for his wife. He had been so intent on scaling Stella's defenses, revealing the woman he knew, obliterating this chemistry between them, that he had ignored the potential consequences.

He felt for her, he always had. Perhaps too much. Her speech tonight had touched him but had also left him deeply conflicted, more aware than ever that he was not the man she thought him to be.

His chest tightened, the guilt in his stomach a heavy weight he'd been carrying so long he was shocked it even registered. He could not afford to play emotional roulette with his wife, not now when he was so close to replacing his father's legacy with a brighter future for Carnelia.

A throb pulsed at his temples. He massaged it with his fingers, attempting to ease the pressure. Allowing this thing between him and his wife to run any deeper couldn't happen. Better to cut off these feelings at the source, stick to the rules they had agreed on.

Stella was already digging holes in his armor, making him question what he was, what he wanted to be. And although she'd been an unquestionably integral presence by his side and would continue to be so, he needed to keep her at an emotional distance. His father was too stark an example of what happened when emotion clouded rational thinking.

Sitting forward, he reached for yet another report he hadn't had time to read. He and his wife were on the same page when it came to this marriage. Deep emotion, love, didn't belong in it.

* * *

Stella awoke alone in the big, luxurious bed, the bright dial on the clock telling her it was far too early to be awake. Three in the morning, in fact. But her husband was.

She sat up and reached for a drink of water. Setting down the glass, she hugged her arms around her knees, a hollow feeling invading her. It didn't surprise her Kostas wasn't there. He never slept well. But the fact that he had taken her apart tonight, then left their wedding bed to work, turned the key on a long-seated feeling of rejection she couldn't quite shake.

I've never wanted a woman more than I wanted you that night, yineka mou, *not since and not now.*

Her stomach clenched, curling into a tight ball. It had been just as beguiling as she'd imagined it would be to discover Kostas wanted her as much as she wanted him. To wipe away his rejection of the past. But on the heels of his expert seduction had also been the knowledge she was exposing herself to new vulnerabilities, *scarier* ones, because now she would have to guard against the adult version of falling in love with him, which could be oh, so much more painful than its predecessor.

Which she would never do. Firming her mouth, she got out of bed, slipped on a robe and went to find her husband rather than ruminate. Ensconced behind the handsome cedar desk in his study, he looked as if what he needed was sleep—days of it.

Fatigue-darkened eyes regarded her as he put down his pen. "You should be sleeping. The send-off breakfast is in a few hours."

"I was thirsty. You were gone." She walked around the desk and perched on the edge closest to him. "Have you always been this way? Not able to sleep?"

"Most of my life, yes."

Because he'd never had any grounding influence to make him feel secure after his grandmother had died. Because the fear and intimidation his father had practiced had likely chased him everywhere, even in his sleep. Her chest grew tight, the soul-deep wound she felt for him growing with every day they spent together. She couldn't change the past, but she could help him now.

She absorbed the lines creasing his brow and mouth, deeper it seemed, in the hours since he'd left her. "What's keeping you up tonight?"

He waved a hand toward the desk. "Half a dozen things."

"But something is making you extra stressed."

He reached out and scooped her off the desk and into his lap. "The election is less than a month away. I have a million things on my mind. I am preoccupied. But now that you are awake," he murmured, gaze dropping to the curves of her breasts the gaping neckline of her robe revealed, "I'd prefer to enjoy you."

Heat invaded her bones, warming her insides, her body recalling the pleasure he could give her. Fighting the hedonistic pull, she curled her fingers around the thick muscle of his biceps. "You promised to share things with me. Let me help."

"I will. Just not tonight." His fingers traced the line of her jaw.

"Did you miss him today? Your father?" So many people had spoken of the làte king, some with a reverence that had blown her away.

"No," he said evenly, "I did not."

She could only imagine the complex feelings Kostas held for his father that must have been unearthed by today. "Your mother's sister was lovely. She seemed to find it bittersweet."

His fingers dropped away from her face. "She didn't want her sister to marry my father. She considered him far too power hungry, too ruthless, but my mother was in love with him."

"It sounded as if she softened him—made him less so."

He nodded. "She was the balancing effect on his personality, the thing that held him in check. When she died, it set off something in his brain, turned loose the controlling side of his psyche, his near psychopathic need for power."

"Too much pain," she said softly.

His eyes turned bleak. "Shortly afterward, his aide found my father in his study with a gun pressed to his head. I think he might have killed himself if the aide hadn't stopped him, made sure my father saw a doctor and received medication for his manic depression. It wasn't a commonly recognized thing then—being a manic depressive—but he clearly was one."

Her heart dipped. "Love can be destructive in so many ways."

"Yes, it can." Amber eyes speared hers. "It's why this arrangement of ours will work—because we based it on our mutual respect for each other, not some illusionary emotion."

She nodded. She was going to keep her feelings out of this. She *was*.

He traced the line of her throat with his fingers. "And very hot sexual chemistry. That we have, too, *moro mou*."

A wave of heat suffused her skin. Nudging the lapel of her robe aside, he closed his fingers over her breast in a possessive movement that stole her breath. She inhaled as his thumb nudged her soft, sensitive areola, sliding over its peak.

"We should go to bed," she said huskily. *Before he obliterated her again.*

"Or not." He covered her mouth with his and bit lightly into her lower lip. "It is our wedding night after all. Creating an heir is...necessary."

Her head spun as his mouth hovered over hers, their breath mingling. *Waiting. Anticipating.* Her insides fisted tight with need. The urge to walk away, to extricate herself before he destroyed more of her defenses, dissolved in a sea of lust.

This *was* her wedding night. Rational thought could come tomorrow.

Gripping her hips, he lifted her, bringing her down so her knees straddled his lap. Eyes on hers, he settled her against his erection covered by the thin pajama bottoms he wore, no barrier to the thick heat that parted her most intimate flesh with possessive intent.

Her gasp split the air. *"Kostas—"*

He rocked against her, sliding his staff against her. Every sensual movement stoked the inferno rising inside of her.

The whisper of his big hand sliding along the sensitive skin of her inner thigh. A stroke of his fingertips against the crease where hip met leg. She squirmed against his touch, flesh on fire.

"Get on me," he murmured in her ear. "I want to take you like this."

Excitement pounding through her veins, she reached down, freed him from the silk that covered him and guided his rigid shaft to her slick flesh. Lowering herself on him, the wide tip of his body pressing against her, a harsh breath escaped her. She froze, absorbing the power of him inside her still tender flesh. Centimeter by centimeter she took him inside her until his big body stretched her muscles so tight she was at the very edge of how much pleasure she could take. Until he touched things that had never been touched before.

Never had she felt so full, so taken, so *possessed*.

"You have all of me now," Kostas said huskily, his voice a hot burn in her ear. "Is that good, *yineka mou*?"

She nodded, past speech. Opening her eyes, she set her hands on the muscular bulk of his shoulders. There was emotion radiating from those fiery, dark eyes as he watched her. He felt *something* for her. But his caution rang in her ear, underlining her own promises to herself. He wasn't ever going to let himself be his father, nor was she ever going to become her mother.

She closed her eyes and focused on the sea of pleasure washing over her. Kostas lifted her off him, then filled her with a delectably slow movement, his erection tantalizing every inch of her. He did it again and again until she dropped her head back and moaned with the pleasure of it.

Cupping her bottom tighter in his palms, he increased his pace, thrusting into her with a deep, intensely erotic focus that sent starbursts of blinding pleasure exploding behind her eyes. He was so big, so hard, he pushed her pleasure beyond anything she'd ever felt, winding her tighter and tighter with each controlled thrust.

"Kostas—" Hot, white lightning radiated out from her center, stiffening her limbs, toes. Whispering hot, heated words in her ear, he pressed his thumb to the tight bundle of nerves at her center, drawing out her orgasm. Another wave of pleasure washed over her, shattering her. Taking her mouth with his, Kostas filled her with deep, deliberate strokes, a low growl escaping his throat as he came.

When the tremors in both of them had subsided, Kostas picked her up and carried her back to bed. This time, as the crisp night air flowed in through the windows, he slept. Head on his chest, she absorbed the tiny victory, then let unconsciousness take her, too.

CHAPTER TEN

A LAVISH WEDDING breakfast had been laid out in the newly renovated dining room of the Marcariokastro for close friends and family leaving Carnelia that day. The warm, charismatic room was a feast for the eye, its recent renovations retaining the original frescos on the walls and ceiling as well as its large, cathedral windows and stunning, intricate dark woodwork.

A massive harvest banquet table ran down the center of the room, the focal point of the space. Dressed this morning with the finest Laskos crystal and china, it was full of fresh flowers and the animated discussion of its occupants, a lively, happy destination. Except for the preoccupation of the bride.

Sitting at one end of the table with Alex, Sofía and Jessie while her new husband was immersed in conversation with her brother at the other end, she had woken up alone in bed again at seven, full of so many conflicting emotions about the night before she could have painted the Akathinian Independence Day parade in about fifty colors of them.

Confusion about her feelings for Kostas. Concern about the pressure he was under. Worry she felt more for him than she'd ever let herself admit.

He had looked as preoccupied as he had the night before when he'd entered the dining room this morning, greeting her with a quick kiss before sitting down with Nik. She knew in her bones something was going on he wasn't telling her.

"So," Alex said archly as Sofía and Jessie went off to find more of the figs and fresh waffles, "how was last night?"

Stella eyed her. "Are you asking me to give you details about my wedding night?"

"Yes." Alex looked unrepentant. "I want to know if that hunk of a man is as good as he looks."

She took a sip of her coffee. Reined in her emotions. "Yes. He is."

Alex's mouth turned down. "That's *all* you're giving me?"

"Yes."

Her sister did not need to know her night with Kostas had been mind-blowingly good. That it had exceeded her expectations in every way. That she was sore in places she'd never been sore before. Because he had also annihilated her defenses, stripped her bare, left her skin feeling too sensitive, her vulnerabilities wide-open.

Alex eyed her. "You okay?"

"Tired."

Her sister chewed on her lip. "Can I say something brutally honest?"

"That depends on what it is."

Alex took a sip of her coffee. Set it down. "Any fool could see you and Kostas have deep feelings for each other. There wasn't a dry eye in the room last night. Try not," she said quietly, eyes on hers, "to sabotage this relationship as you've done every other."

Antagonism lanced through her. "I don't do that."

"Yes, you do."

She put down her cup and shoved it away. "This is a partnership, Alex. I'm too far gone to ever find love. I don't have it in me and neither does Kostas. In that, we are a perfect pair."

Alex frowned. "Don't you think you and Kostas can be different? That you can build on what you have? Aristos is different, *changed*, since us, you've seen that."

"Aristos was crazy about you from the beginning." She sat back in her chair, her gaze flitting over her husband. "Kostas has been molded with so much fear and discipline, taught to keep his emotions inside of him at all costs or he will pay the price. I'm not sure he's ever going to let himself feel. I would be crazy to think I can be the one to change him."

"You don't think I felt the same about Aristos? The press were putting bets on how long our relationship would last, Stella—*bets*—and I was falling in love with him. It was like walking on quicksand."

An apt analogy. "It's not the same," she said with finality. "I believe Kostas cares about me. I believe we can do great things for this country. But that's as far as it goes."

She moved the conversation on to when they would all next get together as her sister-in-law and Jessie came back, plates laden. Better to keep her expectations where they should be and focus instead on what was making her husband so edgy.

The last guest left in the late afternoon. Her husband retreated to his office, murmuring something about a pressing phone call. Missing her family already, Stella sat in the conservatory reading a book.

Her mood disintegrated as the hours went by and her husband remained chained to his desk. She'd signed on to a *partnership*, not to be shunted off to the sidelines while Kostas looked ready to self-destruct.

By nine o'clock she decided enough was enough. Heading upstairs to his study, she knocked, then entered. Kostas looked up from the document he was reviewing, a dark shadow on his jaw, his eyes weary.

"Lypamai." I'm sorry. "I didn't mean to be in here all night."

She fixed her gaze on his. "What's going on, Kostas? What can I help with?"

An unblinking dark stare back. "Election mechanics. Boring but necessary."

"Bore me, then."

"I have to take another call in a few minutes. I'll join you after that."

Heat streaked through her veins at being stonewalled yet again. She turned on her heel and left. In their suite, she undressed and slipped on a more modest ivory negligee than her armor of the night before. Standing in front of the mirror, she brushed her hair with jerky, violent strokes, sending a cloud of electricity up in the air.

Her husband walked in minutes later, tawny gaze fixed on her.

"I thought you had a call."

"I made it quick."

She kept brushing.

"Stella—"

She threw the brush on the dresser and turned to face him. "Talk to me, Kostas, or go back to work."

He folded his arms across his chest. "It's nothing you need to be concerned about."

"I think it is. You're distracted. Your conversation with Nik looked intense."

A weighted silence. "It's Houlis," he said, raking a hand through his hair. "I didn't want to say anything until I had something substantial. I'm receiving intelligence reports he is getting desperate, that he may act before the elections. That phone call was with my security chief putting contingency plans in place."

Ice swept her veins. "He stood there and wished us well yesterday."

"Civility for civility's sake."

She pressed her lips together, a chill chasing up her spine. "Do we have enough support to repel him if he does act?"

"I believe so, but we won't know for sure until the time comes."

Until the times comes. Thee mou. "The pushback you're receiving on your modernization plans... Is that giving Houlis an opening he can exploit?"

That cast-iron look of defiance he'd been wearing for weeks passed across his face. "Perhaps. But it's the right thing to do. Backing down on my plans would only cast my leadership into question. Give Houlis an excuse to pounce."

"Heading into the last weeks of the election with an unhappy public will also do that."

"I am not negotiating this point." Spoken with an iron core.

Diavole, but he was impossible. She gave up. "What are the security plans if something does happen?"

"The plan is to have Houlis and his supporters in jail before a coup can take place. As for you, Nik and I have an extraction plan."

"An *extraction plan*?" Her hands clenched by her sides. "I am the queen of this country, Kostas. I'm not going anywhere if something happens. We are a team. I knew this was a possibility when I signed on."

His expression hardened. "If your life is in danger, you go."

"No."

"Yes."

"We agree to disagree." She held his gaze, a belligerent tilt to her jaw. "I'm tough—as tough as you."

"Yes," he agreed, mouth curving. "You are."

She rested her hands on the edge of the dresser. "You can't carry this alone, Kostas. *You* aren't alone anymore. I am here with you."

Something flickered in his impassive gaze. "All right," he said quietly. "I promise you will know everything I know. But there's nothing more we can do at the moment. We've taken every precaution we can."

She studied the stoic, unfazed look on his strong, *infinitely strong* face. He had a bounty on his head and yet he was unfazed. As if it was just one more obstacle he had to surmount. But this was the man, she reminded herself, whose own father had considered him a threat—to be managed or eliminated. She wondered what kind of an iron interior you would need to have to deal with that. Likely the one that made her husband close himself off when any kind of threat, emotional or physical, put his existence in peril.

She walked over to the bed and sat down. Understanding him, getting through to those locked-away places she needed to know, meant finding out more about how that iron interior had been shaped.

"What was your life like?" she asked. "Being your father's protégé? I can't even conceive of it."

He blinked at the change in subject. "You want to make this relationship work," she said quietly, "let me in, Kostas. I'm trying to understand *you*."

He leaned back against the dresser, long legs splayed out in front of him. "I didn't know any different a life. My studies came first, my grandmother insisted on that.

When I wasn't with her or my tutor, I was with my father, shadowing his steps. Which, in reality, meant I was in the care of his bodyguards and security team."

"You didn't have a nanny?"

"My father didn't believe in them. He said they made you soft."

Of course he had. "What about friends? Were you allowed to have them?"

"The question was did they want to be friends with me. I was the dictator's son, my father was the man who would throw one of their parents in jail one day, or exile another the next. I didn't have a lot of friends as a result of it. Sometimes the children of the palace staff were ordered to play with me when no one else would."

Christe mou. Her heart contracted into a tight ball.

"When my father did spend time with me," he continued, "he was focused on the propaganda—maintaining our legacy. I was his most important disciple. It was all about control and power—over the people and the military junta who backed us. We needed to be impenetrable, stronger than all the rest. Emotion was anathema, a weakness never to be shown."

"Emotion is not a weakness," she countered. "It's a strength. It's how you become a balanced ruler, how you connect with the people. Your grandmother knew that."

"Yes, but she and my grandfather were the exception to the Laskos dynasty. The rest of my ancestors governed with the same fear and intimidation my father did, perhaps to a slightly more moderate degree."

She wrapped her arms around herself, asking the question she wasn't sure she wanted the answer to. "The physical and mental controls he used on you…what were they?"

"It depended on the mood he was in. When he was

on a dark, depressive swing and I'd displeased him, he would ignore me for days, lock me in my room. Sometimes he'd have his henchmen administer whatever punishment they thought fit.

"When he was in his manic phases, he would teach me the skills he thought I needed to master. I was a good shot for my age, for instance, but he wanted me to be the expert marksman he was. If I didn't hit all the targets the first day we went shooting, we'd go back the next until my hands were bruised, my shoulder and arm numb from holding the gun. By the end of that second day I would be hitting those targets. I was so good I rivaled the sniper's shots in the military."

Her insides recoiled. "But not worth the price you paid, surely. No child should have to live up to those unreasonable standards of perfection."

"No," he agreed, with a nod. "I'm merely telling you how I was conditioned. It's not a *way* I choose to be, it's who I am."

She shook her head. "You *feel*, Kostas, just like you've never lost your sense of right and wrong. Just like you never let that monster claim your soul. The passion you have for your people, how overwhelmed with emotion you get every time you see those big crowds that show up for you, the pain you have felt over Athamos's death…it speaks to the depth of feeling you are capable of experiencing. You may *choose* not to allow yourself to feel, but that is another thing entirely."

His mouth twisted. "I feel, but only so far, Stella. Whether it's because I'm not capable of it, or I don't allow it, the end result is the same. Don't expect miracles from me."

"I'm not looking for miracles," she said quietly, "I'm

looking for *you*, Kostas. I know you are in there somewhere."

His face transformed into a blank, unyielding canvas. "Be careful what you wish for. You might not like what you find. You have unrealistic views of me, Stella."

"No." She shook her head. "Perhaps I once did, but not now. Now I realize it was unfair of me to hold you to the standards I did. Unfair of *everyone* to do it. All of us have our human failings—I, more than anyone—but you need to forgive yourself for yours, truly forgive yourself so you can rule with a clear head."

His cheekbones hardened into sharp blades. "I *have* forgiven myself."

She studied the tense set of his big body; how everything seemed to be locked away behind metal bars. "Have you?"

A frozen silence passed. She watched him retreat back into that impenetrable facade of his. "I have more work to do," he said, levering himself away from the dresser. "Don't wait up for me."

Her skin felt too tight and her chest knotted as he walked out of the room. He had needed to hear that, she told herself. He still wasn't thinking clearly about the impact of his aggressive plans on his people and the irreparable harm he was doing himself in the process.

She crawled into bed, physically and mentally exhausted. Kostas's words echoed in her head. *Be careful what you wish for. You might not like what you find. You have unrealistic views of me, Stella.*

Frustration curled her toes. She did *not* have unrealistic expectations of him. Hadn't she just told him that had been unfair of her? Or had Tassos been right? Had Kostas shut down just now because he felt he didn't deserve to be forgiven? That the mistakes he'd made had been unforgivable? Or were there other demons plaguing her husband she would never be privy to?

Curled up in the massive bed with its luxuriously soft silk sheets, she felt chilled, apprehensive and alone—more alone than she'd ever felt in her life. And that was saying something. She'd thought it couldn't get any worse. Perhaps it was because last night with Kostas she'd felt that elusive emotional connection she'd been searching for her entire life.

Where once it had seemed unobtainable, it had been organic with her husband, as if it had just taken the right connection to slot into place—the connection she'd always known was special. Dangerous to her.

The irony of it was undeniable. She'd found that bond with Kostas, the one man she could never explore it with because he wanted no part of it.

An ache wound itself around her heart. What he had told her about his childhood had chilled her, had given her so much more insight into what made him tick. But it had also made her wonder if it wasn't so much that Kostas didn't *want* love, but that he didn't know *what* it was. That he'd been taught it was a weakness, *any* emotion was a weakness, a vulnerability to be exploited.

He was *afraid* of it. If he let someone in, if he admitted his master plan was wrong, if he became anything less than impenetrable, it might all fall apart.

She bit her lip, the salty tang of blood filling her mouth. It might all fall apart anyway if he kept this up; if he refused to bend. But what more could she do than she'd already done? She could only stand by his side, be that unconditional support she knew he needed, ignore the fact that with every day that passed, her true feelings for him were bubbling closer and closer to the surface, threatening to complicate an already too-complicated scenario, the very thing she'd said she'd never do.

CHAPTER ELEVEN

KOSTAS SAT IN his office finishing up work, knowing Stella was likely back from her meeting with the charity, but he elected to push on until dinner. Avoiding his wife was easier than talking about forgiveness and absolution, something he couldn't stomach.

He sat back in his seat and rubbed a hand across his brow. It had been like this since their confrontation in the bedroom. Better to withdraw now and save his wife more pain in the long run, than continue to let her uncover too much of him. Ask for the things he'd warned her he could never give.

A knot tied itself down low. He was hurting Stella with his withdrawal, could see it in her eyes when that tough facade slipped for just a second. Knew it was the last thing he should do to a woman who'd been marginalized by the people she'd loved, who'd experienced enough rejection for a lifetime. But what choice did he have?

He'd tried to make it up to her by allowing her to attend an executive council meeting yesterday as the council prepared to transition to its postelection membership. It had been good to see her light up, to see her brain working frantically as she scribbled notes, had assuaged his guilt just the slightest little bit. But she was looking for more than that from him—she always had been.

Pushing his attention back to his schedule for tomorrow, he perpetuated his avoidance strategy; how that knot twisted itself into a dozen more tangled iterations.

Takis knocked on the door and entered for their final debrief of the day. Working through a few urgent items, they finished with his latest approval ratings that had just come in. The hairs on the back of his neck stood up at the look on his aide's face. Dipping his head, he scanned the numbers. *They were disastrous.* "You're sure these are accurate?"

Takis nodded. "We expanded the poll. The numbers came back the same."

He threw the report on the desk, his heart plummeting. The goodwill he'd amassed since becoming king had vaporized in the wake of that damning editorial and the increasing public discontent that had followed. In fact, he was back to where he'd started. Given they were three and a half weeks away from the elections, it was a disaster.

A disaster his wife had warned him about when he'd shut her down in the bedroom.

"I need time to absorb these." He looked up at his aide. "We'll pick this up in the morning. Discuss a strategy to counter them."

Takis nodded and left. A low, rough word escaped him. How could he have been so shortsighted? Have so vastly misjudged public sentiment as to allow this to happen?

A buzzing feeling settled over him as he attempted to absorb the disaster he'd created. Stella had been right all along. He should have listened to the people, should have compromised, should have found a middle ground. Instead, in his need to be right, to correct his mistakes, to prove to his father, a *dead man*, that he had been wrong about him, that he *would* lead this country to its freedom and self-determination, he had sewn the seeds of his own demise. Given the military an opportunity to hang him.

Rising to his feet, he walked to the bar stored in a hidden cabinet and poured himself a drink. Carrying it to the window, he took a long sip of the smoky, aged whiskey as he looked out at the dark mass of the Ionian Sea spread out below the rugged cliffs that bounded Carnelia.

It was his people's voice he had been fighting for. *Their* voice that needed to be heard. But somewhere along the way he'd forgotten that, the principle swept aside by his blind ambition to save this country.

He took another sip of the whiskey, welcoming its fiery burn down his throat. He struggled with his father's legacy, he knew. Always had. His father had drilled his propaganda into him with such force and regularity, it had been impossible for him to escape his legacy completely.

Confused, caught between what his grandmother was teaching him and what his father was drilling into his head, he had kept his developing thoughts to himself. Closed himself down. Shaped himself into that impenetrable force his father had been. Made himself *unbreakable* in order to survive.

The knot in his gut expanded. His arrogance, his need to become impregnable, had become an obsession, defined his existence. Usually, he managed to keep it under control, rein himself in when he knew he was swinging too far to the other end of the pendulum, but that self-awareness had disintegrated the night Athamos's car had plunged over that cliff on a hot Carnelian night borne of temporary insanity. Then nothing had made sense anymore.

Are you punishing yourself? Stella's words floated

back to him on a quiet mental whisper. *Was he?* He thought he'd put Athamos's death behind him, forgiven himself for his own self-preservation so he could accomplish what he needed to do. But now, as he stared out at the sea from which they had pulled the crown prince's car, the sky as solid a black as it had been the night he and his rival had raced, lit by a sea of stars, he wondered if he had. If Stella was right—that he had made this country his penance… If the one thing he'd never told anyone was the one thing he could never forgive himself for…

A darkness rose up inside of him, an all too familiar, corrosive guilt that had once threatened to eat him alive. He'd been operating on autopilot ever since Athamos's death, determined to lift this country from the ashes, to salvage *something* from the wreck of his life, his wife the only thing that came close to jolting him out of it.

He *had* lost his passion. His idealism. Stella was right. He didn't even recognize himself anymore.

The sight of Athamos's car careening off the road ahead of him filled his head. The squeal of brakes as his rival attempted to steer away from the deadly drop to the cliffs below. The heart-pounding silence that had followed.

His heart pounded in his chest at the memory, so violently he thought his ribs might bruise it. That night was a hell he would never fully escape, a stain on his soul that would forever mark him. But somehow, he knew, he had to find the lessons his guru had preached. Some he knew he'd learned. Others he was sure were yet to come.

It occurred to him as he looked out into the dark, starstrewn night that perhaps part of truly moving on was not becoming what he had been, but what he would *become*. Something better than before. Something worthy of the second chance he'd been given. *Something that would make up for all of it.*

He would make this right.

Stella regarded her husband over the very old, very good bottle of Bordeaux he'd unearthed from the castle's wine cellar, the agony he was clearly in threatening to crush her heart, steal her breath. The emotional knives that had been turning inside of her the entire meal, making it impossible to eat, forced her to finally lay down her fork and knife.

Her husband, who had consumed only a few bites of his meal himself, finally spoke. "Aren't you going to say, 'I told you so'?"

She shook her head. "I think you've punished yourself enough already."

He took a sip of his wine. Pushed the glass back onto the table. "I called Aristos before dinner and asked his advice on how he's dealt with public opposition to his properties."

She nodded, hiding her surprise. A good idea given Aristos had built hotels and casinos all around the world.

"What did he say?"

"He took me through the key interest groups. Told me which ones are key to get onside, which ones we need to court to neutralize the negative factions. He said to make them a part of the decision-making process."

Exactly as she'd counseled. "Good advice. But that will take time. You need something you can execute immediately, something that will turn the tide of public opinion before the elections."

His expression was bleak. "I'm not sure that exists."

"What about a town council?" She voiced the idea that had been percolating ever since that editorial had run. "Get everyone out and let them have their say. Once they've had a chance to offer their opinions, you choose some of those key influencers Aristos was talking about to join your advisory council. Nothing will *happen* before the elections in terms of results, but at least the people will see the promise you are making to listen."

He gave her a skeptical look. "That could end up being a zoo. They will ask for the moon."

"You don't make any promises you can't keep. You agree to compromise."

Kostas was quiet for a long moment, swirling the wine in his glass. "It could," he said finally, "be positioned as me being an empathetic, inclusive leader rather than my backtracking on my plans."

"Yes," she said quietly. "There are worse things than being seen as an empathetic leader."

His gaze sharpened at the gibe. "The people are right to be frustrated. It should never have been allowed to get to this point. *I* should have done something sooner."

Finally, an insight into what was going on in his head. "It took decades of your father's misrule to get the country to this point. You yourself told me how complicated the political situation was before you left. You can't second-guess your decisions."

"It's impossible not to wonder how much damage I could have prevented."

Her heart squeezed. "But it won't solve your problem. You need to leave the past in the past."

He was silent for a long time. When he looked up at her, there was a myriad of emotions blazing in his dark eyes. "Do you really believe that's possible?"

"Yes," she said. "I do. I have these past few weeks and you need to do it, too, Kostas. You're spending so much time trying to prove yourself right, to prove you aren't your father, you've lost the vision that's always guided you, the one your people are looking to you for."

His mouth thinned. "Sometimes I swing too far to the wrong end of the pendulum, I know that. I have a lot of my father in me. In this case I know I have."

"So do the town hall. Open yourself up, show everyone who you are, *prove* to them you are on their side." She shook her head, her voice softening. "I signed up for the man who gave that speech at our engagement party about the self-determination of his people. For *that* man, not *this* one. For the Kostas who sat in that tree and told me he was going to be a more empathetic king."

His gaze fell away from hers. He picked up his wine and took a sip, staring into the flickering candlelight.

"What are you afraid they're going to see?" Her quiet voice brought his head up. "What are you afraid *I'm* going to see, Kostas? Why did you shut down on me the other night?"

He lifted a shoulder. "It would take a psychologist years to get to the bottom of it."

She bit her lip. "And that's it, is it?" she murmured. "Your job is done. Wife secured, wife deconstructed, wife in her appropriate box, the work toward an heir under way? No need to put in any additional effort toward this so-called relationship you wanted?"

The skin across his cheekbones went blade-sharp. "You know it isn't like that."

"Tell me how it *is*, Kostas, because I have no clue."

"We are good together." His amber eyes blazed. "We are making a great team. I *have* made an effort with you. I have told you things I've never told another human being. But you need to know when to pick your battles, when to push and when to stop."

"So you can walk away when it gets hot in a room?

'Be careful what you wish for, Stella, you might not like what you see.' What does that even mean?"

"You're reading too much into it."

"I think I'm not." She fixed her gaze on his. "You asked me to trust you at the beginning of all of this and I have. I've let you in. Now you need to play by the same rules. You are capable of opening up, you've shown that. This marriage hinges on you doing it, because we left the old rules behind us a long time ago. And if you think I can't take it, this is me, Kostas, saving a country with you while a madman waits in the wings."

He gave her a long look. "I know you can take it, Stella, but tonight is not the night." He pushed his chair back, the screech of wood across stone making her wince.

She watched him walk away *again*, her heart dropping. She could only hope she'd given him a potential solution to think through.

Getting to her feet, she went to bed because clearly he needed to process. Pacing their beautiful exposed-stone bedroom, she couldn't settle. The distance between her and Kostas seemed like a million miles apart tonight. Her tumultuous relationship, the tenuous situation they were in coated her mouth with fear.

She should have kept to their original agreement, should never have allowed Kostas to convince her to turn this into a real relationship because exactly what she'd feared would happen was happening. She had allowed her emotions to get involved and Kostas was shutting down, as emotionally unavailable a man as her father ever was.

Her insides twisted into a tight, protective ball. The silence, the palpable strain of dinners in the formal dining room of the palace as her parents had forced her and her siblings to suffer through mandated family dinners, had been toxic, thick with her mother's hurt and anger, her father's ambivalence. Nik used to come up with every excuse in the book to miss them, the atmosphere had been so tense, inventing a stomachache one day, a sprained ankle the next.

When she couldn't stand the empty room one minute longer, she picked up the phone and called Alex. They talked about the latest news, the gossip at home, about the jazz concert Alex was putting on in the spring with the Akathinian legend Nina Karvelas for the youth charity she chaired.

Her sister was over the moon about it, clearly in her element. Stella grew quieter and quieter as the conversation went on.

Alex paused. "You okay?"

She brushed away the tears sliding silently down her cheeks. "Alex," she whispered, "I feel like I'm walking on quicksand."

CHAPTER TWELVE

THE BENTLEY SLID through the night, following the king's town council, the driver taking a complicated series of roads back to the castle as part of the heightened security measures in place given the ongoing threat from the military junta.

Stella rested her head against the seat, heart full to bursting. Her husband had been amazing. With the weight of the world on his shoulders, he had opened himself up to the packed crowd that had filled the auditorium, showing himself as the Kostas she knew, the man who had nurtured infinite dreams, who had enough strength to hold a country together, to build a future for it. The man she had always known he was.

It had not been an easy ride. Frustration, fear and mistrust reigned among Carnelians. They wanted to know they had been heard. Kostas listened to every one of their questions, answered with an insight and compassion that floored her, then took her suggestion and promised to put a handful of representatives on his advisory council so their voices would be heard going forward.

A swell of hope, of rightness, filled her. The café owner had been there. These were her people, too, now. No longer did this country feel foreign and cold to her, devoid of the gilded brightness of her homeland. Instead, she found herself surrounded by a resilience of spirit, a warmth that came from deep within the people's hearts, a courage and fortitude that Carnelians would not see themselves bowed again.

"You were incredible," she told Kostas, breaking the silence. "I think you turned the tide tonight. I think you earned their trust."

He looked over at her, tawny eyes glimmering in the dim light. "It was your idea. Perhaps General Houlis was right. Perhaps you will become the power behind the man."

She searched his face for sarcasm, for some clue to his mood, but there was only the same intensity he'd been wearing all night, dark, unreadable.

"It's you they believe in," she said quietly. "You they needed to see and tonight they did."

Another silence. Kostas looked out the window, the hard lines of his perfect bone structure set in shadow. "I need to thank you," he said finally, looking back at her, "for tonight, for standing by my side. I know it hasn't been easy. I know *I* haven't been easy."

Her heart was a rock in her throat. "You're welcome," she said huskily, past the giant lump. "You aren't the only one who keeps your promises, Kostas. I do. I always do."

He rubbed a palm against the stubble on his jaw, eyes contemplative. "You were right," he said, "about everything that night in my office. I had lost my idealism, my passion, *myself*." His gaze held hers. "You wondered how I dealt with being who I am. How I made sense of it all. I made myself into that impenetrable force my father conditioned me to be. That need to succeed, to win, as you pointed out, translated to every part of my life. It was my defense mechanism when my life became too complicated, when who I *was* became too much. It worked for me, it made sense to me, until," he said quietly, "the night Athamos died. Then nothing made sense anymore."

She bit hard into her lip. "No one can be impenetrable. It's a coping strategy bound to self-destruct."

He nodded. "I did. I walked away. I shattered. But that only made the guilt worse because I had deserted my country. I had *left* them to my father's aggression. My spiritual adviser in Tibet helped me to recover. He taught me my endless drive was destroying me, and it was, clearly. I was determined to learn that lesson, but when I came back, when my father died, the pressure was immense. I shut down. I went on autopilot. The only thing I could see was saving this country, making amends for what I'd done. I didn't see the drive to help my people was becoming as blind an obsession as all the others had been."

"The good intention was there."

"Badly misguided." His gaze darkened. "I *have* been treating this country as my penance, my punishment. Because I haven't truly forgiven myself."

Her throat felt raw. "And have you now?"

"I'm not sure I ever will." A blunt, honest answer. "What I have realized is I've been given a second chance, a chance I plan to make myself worthy of."

Her chest tightened, so tight, it was hard to draw a breath. *The chance Athamos hadn't been given.* It should have ravaged her to hear the consequences of the night put that way, yet instead her emotion for this man and the journey he had been on superseded it.

Reaching out, she laced her fingers through the hand he had resting on the seat. "I think that's a very good plan."

He tightened his fingers around hers. His eyes blazed hot as they met hers. "You are a warrior, Stella, but you are also infinitely wise. You have pushed me when I needed to be pushed and supported me when I refused to listen. I owe you a great deal for that."

"We're a team," she said, eyes stinging with a wet heat. "And don't forget, we made a promise in the tree that day. We said we were going to make this a better world."

"Yes," he said. "So we did."

Kostas returned a couple of calls when they arrived back at the Marcariokastro, then sat back in his seat at his desk in his office, his adrenaline levels slowly easing. He thought maybe Stella was right, that he had turned the tide tonight. But it was his wife's unflinching belief in him that filled his head.

For the first time, he wondered if it was possible to truly forgive himself—for all of it. To leave the past behind. Could he be the flesh-and-blood man he'd never thought himself capable of, love when he'd never known the meaning of the word other than his *yaya*'s affection for a fleeting few years of his life? Be the man Stella needed him to be?

He had married her, he realized, because he'd wanted her, not just because she had been a valuable political tool. Because he'd always wanted her—had walked away from her because he'd feared he wasn't good enough, that he would never live up to her ideals of him.

His wife was right—the point of no return had passed, they had committed themselves to this relationship. He had to make it work. Could she be a part of the second chance he'd been given?

He rubbed his hands over his eyes. Even if he was able to forgive himself for his mistakes, could he ever give Stella what she was asking for? Could he open himself up, or did his conditioning go too deep?

He stared at the pile of work on his desk. Urgent things—things he should attend to. Instead, he turned off the light and stood. Headed toward the irresistible force of nature he no longer had the will to resist.

Stella was brushing her hair in front of the antique mirror when he walked in. She was dressed in a slip of ivory silk, arms raised above her head, her slim body, with its just-enough feminine curves, making his blood heat.

He stood there for a moment, watching her, his body vibrating with need. The blood pounding through his veins flowed into his sex, hardening him with painful precision. Only Stella had ever had this instantaneous, undeniable effect on him. As if by having her, he found his humanity lodged somewhere deep inside him.

She watched him as he walked up behind her and slid his arms around her.

"Kostas…"

He raised one arm up and put a finger to her lips as he pulled her into his pulsing body. "No more talking. Not tonight."

Removing his finger, he set his mouth to the curve of her neck and took a long, deep taste. Her breath hitched, the hand holding the brush dropping to her side. Brushing the tips of his fingers over her nipples, he stroked her into hard peaks. The light imprint he made with his teeth at the pleasure point between her neck and shoulder sent the hairbrush clattering to the dresser.

Watching the pleasure rise over her face in the mirror sent heat to every inch of his skin. He ached to taste, to *devour* the delicate, rosy red peaks that pushed through the translucent silk, so perfectly made, but that wasn't the only part of her he wanted to sample.

Dropping his palm to the shadowed intersection of her

thighs, he pressed the heel of it against her, rotating with sensual, deliberate movements that made her eyes darken.

"I haven't tasted you yet," he murmured in her ear. "I'll bet you're sweet, like honey, Stella."

A red stain moved across her high-boned cheeks. Sliding an arm beneath her knees, he picked her up and carried her to the bed. Depositing her on the rich, dark fabric, he followed her down, pushing up the sexy, transparent fabric she wore to reveal her creamy, golden skin.

Drawing a berry-red nipple into his mouth, he sucked hard, then transferred his attention to the other, until deep, sensual, feminine sounds of pleasure escaped her throat. Sliding down her body, he inhaled her lush, decadent scent, her musky arousal consuming his head.

She watched him as he shackled one of her ankles and bent it back. It left her beautifully, delectably, open to him. The flush in her cheeks deepening, she stayed where she was, motionless, her throat convulsing. Nudging her other thigh outward, he lowered his head and pressed a kiss to the inside of one knee. Continuing the open-mouthed kisses, he worked his way up the silky soft skin of her thigh, feeling the tremors that snaked through her.

When he reached the heart of her, she was rigid, hands buried in his hair, urging him on. But instead of giving her what she wanted, he set his mouth to the back of her other knee and worked his way back up again.

Drunk on the scent of her, he lingered over the aroused heart of her. She arched her hips up in a silent beg. Lowering his head, he swept his tongue over her slick crease. A sharp pant escaped her, her fingers tightening in his hair. *"More."*

"More what?"

"Stop teasing me. *Please.*"

He dipped his head and repeated the tantalizing caress

until she begged in a soft, broken whisper that turned his insides out. Pressing a palm to her stomach, he consumed her in long laps. Her feminine taste was intoxicating, exotic, sinfully good. It made his erection lengthen, thicken.

When she was too close, too soon, he changed strategy, applying a whisper-soft nudge against the tight bundle of nerves at the heart of her. She dug her nails into the sheets, her body so taut she was the perfect, delectable instrument for him to play.

He lifted his head, eyes on hers. "You taste sweet, Stella, as good as I knew you would. Like sweet, hot honey."

She closed her eyes. Clutching the back of his head, she returned him to her. His low growl of approval of her greed sent a shudder through her as it reverberated against her flesh. He picked up speed then, licking her with short, hard strokes designed to take her to the edge. When she begged for him to make her come, he slid one of his fingers inside of her and caressed her deeply. Two. Then he closed his mouth around her and sucked hard. She came with a sharp cry that destroyed the remainder of his self-control.

Rolling off the bed, he stripped his clothes from his body. Coming back to her, he pressed a kiss against her lips, letting her taste the musky, sweet smell of herself on him while he settled himself between her thighs. She wrapped her legs around him, her greed inflaming him with the need to possess her.

She was wet and ready, but she was also tight and delicately feminine. Taking his time, he stroked inside of her, her body easing around him as he went.

A sigh left her lips when he filled her to the hilt. *"Kostas."*

He cupped her jaw in his fingers, pinning his gaze on

hers. "I feel for you, *yineka mou*. More than I should. I always have."

Her gaze deepened to a sparkling amethyst, more violet than blue. Mouth on hers, he thrust inside her, her hips rising to meet his deep, hard strokes. Sliding his tongue against hers, he made love to her mouth as erotically as he took her body, wanting to blow her mind as much as she unbalanced him, took him apart and put him back together again.

She started to shake, come apart beneath him, her sensual response taking him apart. Their lips came together in a darkly sensual connection that destroyed his control. Bowing to the demands of his body, he pumped himself inside of her, taking her faster, harder. She convulsed around him, his name on her lips as her silken flesh gripped him, goaded him into a release that shook his body.

The deep shadows of night swept the bedroom as he curled his wife against him and stroked her silky blond hair. She fell asleep almost instantaneously, the events of the past week having taken a toll, but as exhausted as he was, living on fumes, sleep would not come.

Moonlight sliced across the room, a triangular patch of light shifting on the stone floor as the minutes slid by. His wife wrapped in his arms, the perfection with which they fit together impossible to ignore, he knew he had crossed a line tonight, a line from which he couldn't return.

He wanted everything he'd never had. If there was danger in that leap of faith, if fear fisted his stomach with cold, hard fingers at allowing Stella into a place he'd never allowed anyone, he was willing to risk it.

CHAPTER THIRTEEN

STELLA WALKED OUT of the executive council meeting with Kostas at her side. It had been the final meeting of the council before the body was dissolved and replaced by members selected from the new legislative assembly chosen in tomorrow's elections.

A chance for the current members to earmark issues of importance for the new council to address, it had been a spirited and vocal meeting. Whereas she had sat back and listened in her first meeting, discussing it afterward with Kostas, this time she had spoken up with her ideas about the future, about the injustices Carnelians had suffered and the programs she felt necessary to help them thrive.

Some of what she said was a clear reprimand to those who had managed such portfolios. It sent a ripple through the male-dominated council, but Kostas had backed her up, agreeing the programs she had proposed were necessary.

Hand at her elbow, he helped her into the car, then slid in beside her and shut the door. Her mouth curved as she sat back against the seat. "Your chief of security called me a loose cannon."

"You are."

She flicked him a glance. "Are you angry with me?"

"Obeying protocol is not one of your strong points,

agapi mou. Fortunately," he drawled, a sensual heat in the gaze he swept over her, "you know how to obey when it counts."

Her breath hitched in her throat, her pulse beating a jagged rhythm. He had enjoyed giving her orders when he'd taken her to bed last night. Stark, sexually explicit orders that had made it more exciting than it had ever been before. Caught up in the pleasure he was giving her, she'd obeyed every single one of them.

With the swiftness of a cat, he caught an arm around her waist and pulled her onto his lap.

"Kostas," she breathed, "we're in the car."

"Which has blacked-out windows and a privacy screen." His fingers curved around her neck to bring her mouth down to his. "You in power mode puts me in an indecent frame of mind."

His kiss was hard, hot and possessive. She sighed and melted into him, returning the kiss with the responsiveness he demanded. Flicking his tongue over the seam of her lips, he insisted on entry, deepening the kiss with slow, sweet strokes.

Her fingers curled into his shirt. Every touch, every stroke, every lick, carnal and earthy, pulled her deeper and deeper into the vortex that was Kostas. Somewhere along the way, she realized hazily, her desire to be impenetrable had been exposed as the front it was, for what she really wanted—the love of this man.

It stole her breath as she broke the kiss and leaned back, studying the harsh set of his jaw, how he was hard lines and strength everywhere except in his eyes at that moment. His feelings for her were written across them. She just had no idea how deep they ran.

Perhaps he might come to love her in time. Maybe it was possible. Maybe they could learn to do this together. Or maybe she was the biggest fool on the planet for thinking such self-destructive thoughts when he'd clearly warned her off.

"What?" Kostas smoothed a thumb over her jaw.

She breathed deep. Attempted to stem the panic crawling up her spine for this wasn't the only thing she had to face today.

"Later," she murmured, sliding off his lap.

When they arrived at the castle, Stella went directly upstairs to her bedroom while Kostas headed to his office to work. The purchase Page had made was tucked away in the drawer as requested. Her heart was a hammer in her chest as she pulled the two pregnancy tests out of the bag. Two—just to make sure—although she already knew the answer.

Her breasts were tender, her mood even more jumbled this past week, her psyche somehow more fragile. Kostas was so damn virile, she'd *expected* it, but nothing could really have prepared her for the two plus signs that stared back at her a few moments later.

An heir for Carnelia. What the country had been waiting for… Head buzzing, she tossed the evidence into the trash can and sat down on the antique stool. It had been the goal, of course, to conceive Kostas's heir. With Kostas's approval ratings having risen dramatically since the town hall, it was the last piece of the puzzle to slide into place.

Her hands clenched so tight she could feel her nails digging into her skin. She knew it was good—*wonderful*—news. Fear still clamped her chest like a vise. Could she be a good mother after her own childhood? Could she and Kostas give their children the unconditional love and acceptance they'd never had? Ensure they never knew the loneliness and isolation that had marked both their early years? Would her relationship with Kostas continue to flourish so they could be those parents they'd never had?

She dropped her head into her hands as the room spun around her. Giving that last piece of herself to Kostas, making a leap of faith that he could someday learn to love, meant letting go of the painful experiences that had shaped her life and trusting the future could be different.

Alex had been right. She'd sabotaged every relationship she'd been in because she'd been afraid of getting hurt. Perhaps it was time to stop letting the past rule her. Hadn't she preached the same to her husband? Shouldn't she be brave enough to do it, too? Or was she setting herself up to repeat history in the most painful of ways?

"There is a lieutenant from the navy here to see you, Your Highness."

Kostas looked up from the report he'd been scanning. Frowned. The navy was Houlis's domain. "He's been screened?"

"Yes. He said it was a personal matter. He wouldn't discuss it with me."

A personal matter? Curiosity pulled at his insides. "*Kala.* Send him in."

A young man in his late twenties walked in, his short, buzzed haircut instantly marking him military. He introduced himself as Lieutenant Miles Colonomos. Kostas returned his greeting and waved him into the chair opposite his.

"How can I help you?"

The lieutenant reached into his pocket and withdrew a box. He set it on the desk and pushed it toward Kostas. "One of my men was doing a routine check on the western perimeter when he found these caught on a rock at the base of the cliffs."

Kostas's heart was a knot in his throat and he didn't know why. Athamos's car had gone over the cliffs on the western side of the island, but the crown prince's car had been the only thing they'd ever been able to find, Athamos's body swept away by the strong currents.

He pulled the box toward him and closed his fingers over the cover. Lifting it, he saw two oblong, flat aluminum discs attached to a chain of the same material. His brain flatlined. *Dog tags.* The piece of identification pilots wore in case they were lost in combat.

They all bore a soldier's first and last names, their social security number, blood type and religion. Came in twos so that one could be removed from a dead man's body to notify his family of his death should the body need to remain behind.

The tags in the box were wrong side up. His gaze blurred and his hand trembled as he flipped one over, an unnecessary action because he knew whose they were.

Athamos Constantinides
102300
Blood Type: O
Religion: Greek Orthodox

He sat there, motionless, staring at the two pieces of metal, jagged glass lining his throat. "Anything else?" he asked, his voice a sharp rasp. "Did your diver find anything else?"

The officer shook his head. "The tags must have been ripped from the prince's body during the fall. They were lodged in a crevice. The only reason we found them was the rock had shifted."

He nodded. They had scoured the waters for days, *weeks*, looking for Athamos's body to give his family closure, but they'd never been able to provide it. Now, he thought, his gut twisting, they would have it.

"Efharisto." Thank you. He nodded at the officer. "Please keep the information to yourself. The family must be notified."

The other man nodded and took his leave. Rising from his chair, Kostas walked to the window and attempted to breathe past the tightness in his chest. He couldn't bring Athamos back, he had accepted that, but giving his dog tags to Stella was something else entirely.

Spreading his palm wide against the glass, he absorbed the shame that flooded through him. For his recklessness that night. For his weakness in not going to Athamos's family immediately and telling the story. For thinking he could hide the truth from his wife as to who he was.

For he had to tell her. This was a sign, a reminder that the last piece of the truth still lay between them. It had been foolish of him to think he could keep it from her, he realized, heart sinking. It would lie there forever, festering, rearing its ugly head whenever his demons got the better of him, and that couldn't happen, not when he was sure he loved his wife. That he had always loved Stella.

She had transformed from willful princess to a powerful, empathetic queen in front of his eyes. She had slain every dragon alongside him. Now he had to hope they were strong enough to weather this storm together or he would lose the one woman who meant everything to him.

Stella paced the floor of the conservatory, waiting for Kostas's meeting to end.

Takis finally appeared in the doorway after she'd nearly worn out the floor. "His Highness's guest is gone."

"Efharisto."

Making her way down the stone corridor that led across the castle to the visitor's wing, she walked into the king's offices. Tapping lightly on the door, she opened it at her husband's command to enter. The minute she looked at Kostas's face she knew something was wrong. *Something was very, very wrong.*

Her news fell to the wayside as she came to a halt in front of his desk. "What is it?"

He held out a hand. "Come here."

She skirted her way around the desk and slid onto his lap. Taking her hand, he pressed a kiss to her palm. "I need to show you something."

Her heart was a drumbeat in her throat. "Is it the military?"

"No. Everything's fine."

Letting go of her hand, he reached for the small, black box sitting on his desk and handed it to her. "A navy diver found this today."

"A navy diver?" She frowned. "What is it?"

"Open the box."

The edge to his voice turned her blood to ice. Hands shaking, she opened the box. Knew immediately what was inside because she'd seen Athamos wearing them. *Dog tags.* Her gaze flew over the two pieces of metal, fingers clenching the box so tight her knuckles went white.

Athamos. *They were Athamos's dog tags.* Her hand flew to her mouth. "You found him?"

"No." He shook his head. "I'm sorry, *agapimeni*, we didn't find him. These must have been torn from him when the car went over the cliff."

Her heart convulsed. Picking up the two pieces of metal, she cradled them in her palm. They were cold. *Final.*

Heat stung the back of her eyes, the truth washing over her like an undeniable force. This…*this* was all she was ever going to have of her brother.

She looked up at her husband. "He's never coming back."

Such dark, dark emotion reflected back at her. "No."

Moisture streaked down her cheeks. Kostas rested his chin on her head and held her as she cried, tears soaking his shirt. It seemed as if she cried for a very long time.

"Thank you," she murmured when the tears had slowed to a crawl. "At least we have a piece of him. It's more than we ever thought we'd have."

Kostas was silent. The tenseness enveloping him straightened her spine. "What?" she whispered. "What is it?"

"I need to tell you something."

The hairs on the back of her neck rose. Somehow she knew another blow was coming and she wasn't sure if she could take it.

His gaze captured hers. "The night Athamos and I raced, I was furious with my father for his behavior, worried about what damage he would do before I could take control, antagonized I could do nothing about it, tortured by the decisions in front of me.

"Cassandra," he continued, "is a beautiful woman. Both Athamos and I wanted her. Athamos fell hard, though, harder than I'd ever seen him fall for a woman. He was in love with her, but I knew Cassandra was interested in me, maybe even in love with me. I should have let the two of them be, but my need to blow off some steam, my need to *win*, was stronger."

She pressed a hand to her mouth, bile stinging the back of her throat. "Kostas, no—"

"Yes." His voice was a harsh whip against her skin. "You need to know the truth. You need to know all of it."

She shoved a hand against his chest, needing him to stop, needing not to hear this right now because everything—*everything*—depended on them making this marriage work. He held her there, his arm an iron band around her waist.

"It was a game for me, Stella. To prove I could have her." His words were like grenades, blowing up in her face. "Athamos had become my friend and yet I didn't care. I goaded him, ensured he would take the challenge. *I* was responsible for his death."

She put her hands up to shield herself from the blows, from *more*, but he was done, staring at her with jagged pain in his eyes.

"Why?" she whispered. "Why are you telling me this now?"

"Because keeping this from you would have destroyed me. Because *we* need to have a future free of the past."

"Destroyed *you*?" She shoved a hand at his chest. This time she caught him unaware and managed to scramble off his lap before he caught her. She stood in front of him, limbs shaking. "You challenged my brother to a race when you *knew* he was in love with the woman you were playing with. You stole his life from me, Kostas."

Naked pain crawled across his face. "Don't you think I wish I had been the one to have gone over that cliff? Don't you think this hasn't nearly driven me mad, Stella? But I can't do that. I can't take his place. I can't bring back the dead. I can only forgive myself as you yourself said and do the best I can to make something out of all of this. Something good."

She closed her eyes because rational speech wasn't

penetrating the grief surrounding her. All she could feel was the spear of ice he'd shoved through her heart.

Kostas walked around the desk, stopping a step away from her. "We have something special, Stella, something rare. We always have. Our marriage was a key alliance, yes, but you know it was because I wanted you. I've always wanted you."

Red rose in front of her eyes. *"Wanted?"* She spat the word at him. "The game has never ended, has it? It never will. It's the only thing you know."

He shook his head. "It's not a game. This thing between us is real, you know it is."

The pain lancing her heart dug deeper. "I gave you so many opportunities to tell me the truth. I was *begging* for it and still you said nothing. How can I believe anything you say?"

"Because I love you."

She recoiled, feeling as if she'd been sucker punched. "You don't know how to love anyone, Kostas. You said so yourself."

His gaze was steady. "I do love you. I have always loved you."

She shook her head. "You just decimated that."

"Stella—"

Turning on her heel, she flew out of the room and headed for the hallway to the other wing, footsteps echoing a solitary tread on the stone floor.

Tears rolling down her face, she dashed them away with her fist as she sidestepped a maid and took the stairs to the royal wing. Staff dotted the hallways as they went about their afternoon tasks, so she changed direction and took the back stairwell to the top of the castle. Climbing the extremely old, dank set of stone steps, she emerged on the palace ramparts, a sweeping view of the mountains to her right, the cliffs and coastline to her left.

She wasn't sure how long she sat on the stone bench, knees to her chest, arms wrapped around them as the high sun of midafternoon faded into a dusky pink-and-orange sunset. It was the type the tourists went gaga over, one that would bring them here in droves when Kostas's developments came to fruition, but it barely penetrated the ice that surrounded her heart.

There were no more puzzles now, no more mysteries. Her brother, who had never loved easily, had been mad about Cassandra Liatos, and in typical, stubborn Athamos fashion had refused to give up. Perhaps he had known Cassandra was in love with Kostas and pursued her anyway, perhaps he hadn't. The only thing that was certain was that the two people who could have put a stop to the madness—Cassandra and Kostas—had not.

She stared out at the foam-capped waves as they crashed against the cliffs where her brother's car had gone over the edge. It was true, Athamos had also been responsible for his actions that night, but Kostas, however, bore the biggest blame of all because his actions had been premeditated. He had wanted to win and to hell with the consequences.

She understood he could never have predicted what would have happened that night, understood the frustration that had driven his rash behavior, *believed* his grief over it had nearly shattered him. But how could she be sure, given her husband's ruthless determination to save this country, that she was not simply the pawn she'd always feared she was? That that was all she was to him?

Because, a tiny mental whisper said, *he didn't have to tell you*. He could have carried the truth of that night to his grave and no one would have been the wiser. No one would have gotten hurt. But he hadn't.

Be careful what you wish for. You might not like what you find.

He had been agonizing over this. Tortured by it. Suddenly, it all made sense. He had been doing exactly what she'd asked for just now, telling her the whole truth—the deepest, darkest part of him. Because he wanted them to work.

In her heart she knew he'd meant everything he'd said, that this had been the thing holding him back all along. But could she trust what he had said? That the man who'd professed he wasn't capable of love had discovered he could?

CHAPTER FOURTEEN

KOSTAS SLEPT EVEN less than usual. The pink fingers of dawn were creeping across the sky when he got out of bed and dressed, his movements slow and deliberate as he donned a dark suit and a silver-gray tie.

Today his future would be decided in the first elections in Carnelia's history. His *and* Stella's future.

His wife had chosen to sleep in one of the adjoining bedrooms last night after telling him she needed space. Relieved she had not walked out, left him, he had given her the space she needed, resisting his urge to *fix*.

His heart beat a thick rhythm in his chest as he did up his cuff links, fingers feeling too clumsy for the task. He'd thought he'd been done with the big, life-changing mistakes, but not telling Stella the full truth about Athamos, not taking the opportunities she'd given him, was going to haunt him for a very long time.

For a man who'd always thought himself incapable of love, it had been a sin of omission he could live with. But for one who'd realized he could, it was blind stupidity of the highest order.

He drank an espresso as he went through his day with Takis, stomach pacing like a tiger in a cage. He was scheduled to meet with the chief administrator of the elections first thing this morning before visiting key polling stations to greet Carnelians as they came to the polls. His wife had still not appeared when he left the castle at eight thirty. Dust in his mouth, gravel in his throat, his heart in no way right, he got into the Bentley and made the drive into town.

He was exiting the government building after his meeting with the administrator when gunfire cracked around him.

Stella rose after a long, sleepless night. Her mind, however, was clear. She loved Kostas. She wasn't going to let him stand alone today, not after everything they'd been through.

She dressed in dark pants, a white blouse and a scarf done in vivid blues and reds. Unwilling to wait the whole day until her husband's return, she found Darius and asked him to drive her into town. She'd do some of the polling station visits with him.

Darius brought the car to a halt at the base of the front steps. The crowds from the night of her engagement party flashed through her head. The night had been full of such hope. Would today be the culmination of it all? The realization of her husband's dreams? Or would his mistakes prove fatal?

Darius was talking into that eternally present wireless headset of his, a bud in his ear and a microphone embedded in his shirt. Rather than sit in the car, she waited, foot tapping, hand against the car. It was a beautiful day. A day for new beginnings.

Her bodyguard had his serious look on now, one that put her senses on alert. Moving closer, she listened as he spoke rapidly into the mouthpiece. She caught only every second or third word, but she heard enough to make her blood turn to ice.

Gunfire. Junta. Not secure.

Firing off a couple of rapid-fire sentences, her body-guard cut off the call. "You need to get inside *now*."

"Why? What—" A shout from the palace gates stole her attention. They were closing them, the thick, iron doors swinging shut.

"Darius—what's going on?"

"The military. They're attempting to seize control."

Her heart jumped into her mouth. "Kostas?"

"He was exiting the building when it happened. I can't get Henri on the phone. Everything's on lockdown."

Cold fingers clamped down on her spine. She headed around the car to the passenger seat. "We need to go there."

Darius came after her. "You need to follow protocol and get inside *now*."

She glared at him. "I don't give a damn about protocol. We are going there."

Darius, now toe to toe with her, shook his head. "I have an extraction plan to follow. Get inside."

She reached for his car keys, heart pounding, perspiration breaking out on her forehead. He evaded her, a dark look on his face as he pocketed his keys.

"Darius," she yelled, "something could have happened to him. Take me there."

He caught hold of her like the precision machine he was and slung her over his shoulder. She pounded on his shoulders, fury raging through her.

"I am the queen of this country. *Christe mou*, Darius. Put me down."

He didn't put her down until they were inside the castle, doors locked behind them. Takis met them in the entrance hall.

"Any news on Kostas?" Darius asked.

The old man shook his head.

Darius got on his phone again. The words *extraction* and *bird* filtered through her consciousness, but she wasn't really listening. *What if Kostas had been shot? Why wasn't Henri answering his phone?*

Her bodyguard ended the call and turned to her. "The helicopter will be here in minutes. Get your stuff."

Her knees felt weak. "I told you, I'm not going anywhere."

"Your husband and brother gave me orders, Stella. If I don't get you out of here *now*, our window of opportunity closes."

"Then let it." She crossed her arms over her chest. "I'm not going. Kostas was prepared for this. Our troops will come through. It will be fine."

Darius turned the air blue. Pulling out her mobile, she punched in Nik's number. He answered on the second ring. "You okay?"

She nodded, then realized he couldn't see her. "Yes. They've attacked the government building."

"I know. I'm on the other line with my contact on the ground. The chopper is minutes away."

"I'm not leaving him, Nik." Her hand clutched her mobile so tight it nearly cut off her circulation.

"Stella." Her brother's voice hardened. "Kostas and I agreed on this. Anarchy could ensue if Houlis takes control. Get on the helicopter and come home."

"Listen. To. Me." She said the words slowly, with control. "I am not leaving him. I love him. So tell me what to do."

"Stella." Nik used his most persuasive voice. "I know you love him. You still need to get the hell out of there and let Kostas straighten this out."

"No."

A harsh sigh in her ear. "If anything happens to you…"

"Nothing is going to happen to me *or* Kostas," she said fiercely. "I told him I was going to stay by his side and I will. Sofía wouldn't leave you in the same position, you know she wouldn't."

Silence. "*Kala.* We've sent in commandos to help Kostas and his men. I'll keep you updated as I know anything. Keep your damn phone on and make sure I know you're okay."

"Okay."

She hung up. Felt herself die a little more as the minutes and hours stretched by with no news. Finally, just after noon, a call came in from Kostas's chief of security. The king was fine, his security forces had apprehended General Houlis and the rest of the insurgents and placed them in jail. According to the security chief, key factions allied to Houlis had deserted him in the final hours.

Stella's knees nearly gave way. Page made her sit and eat something. It was four o'clock before her husband walked in the door, dark-shadowed and hollow-eyed. She stood, so relieved to see him in the flesh, unharmed, her knees did give way. A curse on his lips, Kostas ate up the distance between them and caught her in his arms.

"You should have left." Sliding an arm beneath her knees, he picked her up.

"I promised you I wouldn't. We're a team." She buried her mouth in his throat, drinking in the dark, masculine scent of him, ensuring herself he really was in one piece.

Kostas muttered something to Takis, then carried her into the conservatory. Sitting down on one of the sofas, he cradled her in his arms.

She pulled back so she could see him. "I love you. I was coming to tell you that when Darius picked me up and locked me inside."

"It's the only way to control you. You still can't follow protocol." His low, raspy voice was filled with emotion as he smoothed his thumbs across her face.

"Did you hear what I said? I love you."

"Yes." His gaze darkened. "Does that mean you forgive me?"

"If you promise me there are no other secrets. That we can move on with a blank slate. That you will *talk* to me. Always, about anything."

He nodded, pressing a long, hard kiss to her lips. When he drew back, the pain in his eyes tore at her heart. "What happened that night with Athamos is a stain on my soul, Stella. I didn't think I deserved to be forgiven, not by myself and certainly not by you. I thought I could protect both of us by suggesting we have a marriage of convenience, one that involved only sex and affection, that never went too deep, because then I would never have to hurt you. What I didn't factor into the equation was the fact that my feelings for you have always run too deep. It was never going to work."

"You should have told me. On this we were clear, Kostas. Trust, transparency and complete honesty were what we agreed on."

"I was afraid you would walk away." He shook his head. "You're right, I know, but I never thought it would be a problem. I thought it would never go that far. Then you started shooting sparks, forcing me to feel alive, forcing me to acknowledge my past and my emotions. Then I fell in love with you and I couldn't risk telling you because I knew you would hate me."

She bit her lip. "Is that it? Is that all I need to know? I can do this, Kostas, but there can't be any more land mines to blow us apart."

A bleak cast entered his gaze. "I can't promise the

pieces of me that emerge—*who* I am—will be pretty. There is too much ugliness in my past. But that was the whole truth I told you. There are no more secrets."

"Then we can do this." She curved her fingers around his nape and brought his mouth down to hers in a long, promise-filled kiss. It lasted for what seemed like forever, but not nearly long enough.

"You make me want to be things I never thought I could be," Kostas said huskily, resting his forehead against hers. "You make me want things I thought I could never have. You always have."

Her heart fell apart. "Speaking of which," she whispered, "I have something to tell you."

His face went silent, still. "You're pregnant?"

Her brows drew together. "How do you know?"

"I suspected when you didn't drink wine at dinner the other night, but you didn't say anything, so I figured I was wrong."

"I hadn't done the test. I did two, actually. Both came back positive."

"And you stayed here today?" His stillness dissolved in a blaze of pure emotion. "Stella, *Christe mou*, what were you thinking?"

"That we are doing this together, you and I, like we promised." She lifted her chin. "And we will, as soon as the election results come in."

He smiled. "Confident as always, *yineka mou*."

"I believe in you." She brushed a kiss against his mouth. "When did you know you loved me?"

"The day I saw you in that tree."

Stella stood with Kostas on the steps of the new government building that evening, her hand in his as the election results were confirmed. A roar went up in the crowd assembled. The monarchy would remain in Carnelia, with Kostas as head of the new government, leading an elected national assembly. A new age had begun, ending the darkest period in the tiny Mediterranean country's history.

Stella stood on tiptoe and kissed her king. "Whoops," she said when she was done, lips against his. "Was that a break in protocol?"

"As if you care." Cupping the back of her head, Kostas gave the crowd a kiss to remember.

The rebel princess had become a queen. This time her wings would not be clipped. Not with this man at her side.

* * * * *

In case you missed them,
the other stories in Jennifer Hayward's
KINGDOMS & CROWNS *trilogy*
are available now!

CARRYING THE KING'S PRIDE
CLAIMING THE ROYAL INNOCENT

MILLS & BOON®

MODERN™

POWER, PASSION AND IRRESISTIBLE TEMPTATION

0816/01